Christmas Cupid
By

Roxy Wilson

BLURB

Janay Riley can always spot a match made in relationship heaven, but, when it comes to her own love life, she hasn't quite found her perfect match. Although her love life isn't thriving, her business is growing and, for now, that's enough for her.

When long-time friend and admirer, Randy 'Fitz' Fitzgerald finally wants to make his feelings for her known, the consummate matchmaker springs into action. Thinking that he's asking for assistance, Janay sets out to find him the perfect match.

As part of Fitz's ploy, he adds fuel to the fire by seeking advice about his dating woes. That seemingly innocent conversation between friends results in a night neither he nor Janay will soon forget.

Will Fitz's game ruin any chance he has of having a relationship with Janay, or will love conquer all and bring the two long-time friends together this Christmas?

ALL RIGHTS RESERVED

This is a work of fiction. All characters, places, businesses, and incidents are from the author's imagination, or they are used fictitiously and are definitely fictionalized. Any trademarks or pictures herein are not authorized by the trademark owners and do not in any way mean the work is sponsored by or associated with the trademark owners. Any trademarks or pictures used are specifically in a descriptive capacity.

No portion of this book may be reproduced in any form (electronic or print) without permission from the author. Please do not participate in piracy or violating the author's rights.

Text copyright © 2019 Roxy Wilson
All Rights Reserved

Chapter One

The night was young. Janay Riley swiped her beer from the countertop and took a sip as she surveyed the milieu at the bar. The tall, heavy Christmas tree glowed with twinkling lights. Christmas may still be three weeks away, but the festive season had already begun. She could feel the excitement in the air, the sense of anticipation and good cheer. Buoyed by it, surrounded by a bunch of friends and buffeted by the fast music that pumped out of the speakers, she felt great. After a hard day's work at her and her sisters' company, Grand Events, she liked hanging out with her friends in one of the thousands of hot spots that dotted the city.

New York was her favorite place to be, especially at this time of the year. Her work was fantastic. She had a great coterie of friends. Janay wasn't the sort to get bogged down by anything; she loved her life and enjoyed it to the fullest.

The bar seemed to be hopping. Someone tapped her on the shoulder.

"Kiera!" She hugged the cherubic blonde girl whom she met more than six months ago. "So glad you could make it." Then she swiveled to the rest of the group. "Hey, everyone! This is my friend, Kiera." Amidst the friends' enthusiastic greeting she continued, "She's an aspiring interior decorator, currently working with James Rush's Beautiful Homes." Janay wriggled her eyebrows at Mason, a doctor she'd known for the past five years. Having gushed praises of Kiera to him, she now sat back to see if her hunch would be right.

"Would you like something to drink?" Mason asked Kiera.

"Sure. A martini would be nice." Kiera squirmed on the stool when Janay pinched her on her arm. "Why don't I go and order with you?" Kiera added hastily, as she rubbed the spot.

The group watched as Mason and Kiera sauntered off to place their orders.

Jason chuckled. "Jan, don't tell me this is another one of your matchmaking schemes?"

"Hey! I'm fairly good at it. I'm now fresh off the success of Cheyanne and Malick's engagement party. Let me tell you, I've got an uncanny eye for this." She glanced at the retreating couple as they meandered their way through the bar. "Mason and Kiera are perfect for each other. They're both slightly geeky." She chuckled as she ticked off their traits with her fingers. "Both love animals," she said as she touched her thumb.

"They're both an only child." She tapped her index finger. "They want to have at least two or three kids one day and they're ready for a serious, long-term relationship." She ticked off two more fingers. "I can just sense it..." She glanced up at the ceiling as if she were actually having an epiphany. "Just wait and see."

"What are we waiting to see?"

Janay stared into the startling dove-gray eyes of her best friend. Randy Fitzgerald—Fitz, to no one else, but her—and she completed their high school together and later, he went to law school. Despite the fact that he moved out of state, they stayed in touch. But two years ago, he came back to New York and they resumed their friendship as if seven years hadn't passed in between. "In a matter of a few days, you'll see the result of my latest matchmaking efforts," she explained, as the group of friends shifted a little, so Fitz could join them around the same table.

"Ahhh, Janay!" he groaned. "You're still at it even after Chuck and Lori broke up?"

Janay grimaced. Trust him to bring that up! "That was a severe blow," she admitted with a quick toss of her hair. "But it wasn't my fault that they weren't smart enough to see how good they were together."

"Oh, yeah?" Fitz rolled his eyes. "Except that they nearly killed each other during one of their fights."

"Hey, if Chuck couldn't keep it zipped up?" She shrugged. "No woman wants a guy who can't be faithful to her." She raised a hand before Fitz could open his mouth to comment again, "Okay, fine. I'll accept that they weren't one of my greatest achievements. But you've got to admit, my success rate is good, damn good if you ask me."

"You only do this because when they get engaged or married, they come to Riley's Grand Events to give you some business," Fitz joked.

She laughed as she gave his arm a playful punch. "You devil! That's not why I do it and you know it. I've been doing this since high school. Don't you remember—?"

He placed his index finger on his mouth. "Hush, now! I don't think I could take another lecture about all the people who've been showered with eternal love because of your matchmaking skills." He extended his arm to her. "Come and dance with me. I love this song."

Janay picked up her beer bottle, gulped down the remnants of her beer and set the bottle on the table. Since she loved to dance, it was an offer she could hardly refuse. "Okay. I'll show you some moves, man."

"Been taking dance lessons again?" he teased.

"Zumba is for exercise." She held her chin high as he led her on to the floor.

One thing about Fitz; he was a hunk of a man. With his broad shoulders, narrow waist and long legs, he could have been a model. Instead, he'd become a hotshot lawyer who was fast making a name for himself. Becoming a partner in his law firm was his dream.

She felt quite confident that he could do it. For as long as she'd known him, he knew what he wanted and how to get it. He always had a plan. And no matter what came his way, he made it work for him.

More than anything else, he was a great guy. It always amazed her to see that he was still single. Oh yeah, sure...he dated women, but there wasn't any serious relationship for a long time. What could be the reason for it? She watched him as he danced. He sure did have moves, for a white guy—and that's why stereotyping others because of perceived differences was wrong on so many levels. Case in point, she knew some black guys who seemed to have two left feet—or two right feet for that matter—when they were on the dance floor. As for Fitz? The man knew how to move his body to get the maximum mileage. There were a lot of women who were staring at him. While they danced together, completely in tune with each other's rhythm, she wondered why he didn't have his dream girl yet. Probably, because he was too choosy.

"What are you thinking about?"

"Just wondering why you haven't hooked up with anyone as yet?" She twirled while he turned her around. When she came back into his arms, her breasts pushed against his chest. Immediately, a frizzle of desire tingled its way up her spine.

And why the hell not?

He's a hot guy—and she wasn't exactly dead. But he was her friend. And not just *a* friend. He is *the* friend. She relied on him a lot to set her right when she lost her direction. Always there when she needed him. There were plenty of times when she cried on his shoulder; after a break up, before a hook up, when her aunt died and when her parents moved away.

Fitz had always been an important pillar in her support system and she wasn't going to lose him just because she couldn't keep her hormones under control. She ignored the need pulsating inside her to push her body against him. That wouldn't do at all.

No way!

"I just haven't found the right person," he muttered. He gestured towards Kiera and Mason who were strolling out onto the patio together to be separate from the rest of the group. "Looks like your latest effort may be quite a success."

Janay caught Kiera's eyes and the woman waved with a smile. Janay gave Kiera the thumbs-up sign. She turned back to face Fitz. "Way to go, Kiera." She chuckled.

"I suppose, we'll never hear the end of this now." Fitz groaned and pulled her into his arms.

For a moment, his chin rested on her hair and she could've sworn that she heard him taking a deep breath. For the first time, it mattered to her if he loved the scent of her hair and her skin.

Then they separated. The song changed and Fitz led her back to the table.

"I'll reserve judgment on Mason and Kiera's relationship until it's a few weeks old," she told him as she sat. "You want another beer? I can handle one more, before we leave."

"No," Fitz replied. "Allow me!" He went to order their drinks. A few minutes later, he returned and put her bottle on the table. "So, what's the news?" He took the seat opposite to her. "I heard your sister Brielle is hitching up again."

"Yep!" She rolled her eyes. "With Toby of all the people!"

Fitz frowned. "You don't like him? I remember when they were married. You couldn't stop talking about what a cool guy he was. You used to sing his praises as if he were a saint."

Just one more thing she loved about Fitz. They had a history. He knew everything about her family and was on friendly terms with her sisters...so easy to talk to him. "Oh, I like him well enough," she admitted. "Always did. He's a great guy, but they both went through such upheavals that I just hope all goes well this time around."

"I'm sure it will. Brielle is sensible. If she's taking a chance with him again, it means it's the right thing to do."

"People make stupid mistakes in love," Janay noted. Was she imagining it or did his gray eyes have streaks of blue in them? Why didn't she ever notice before? "Oh! Look at me talk. I should withhold my judgment. Actually, I'm quite fond of Toby. He's a gem. It's just the over-protective sister in me talking." She chuckled. "You mess with one Riley sister, you mess with all of them."

He took a swig from his bottle. "When are they getting married?"

"In February and you're invited. In fact, if you're free, you could be my date. I'm not seeing anyone right now, and I don't want to take a loser to my sister's wedding."

"Why? You're not going out with that what's-his-name-the-egotistic-brat anymore?" He referred to her last boyfriend, an investment banker. "Thought you guys were going strong."

She snorted. "We broke up two weeks ago. He was getting on my nerves. I mean, if he can't trust me, what's the point of going out?"

"Trust is very important in a relationship," Sandra, another mutual friend chimed in while listening to their conversation. "If a man doesn't have a hundred percent faith in me, there's no point being with him."

"Easy for you to say," Fitz retorted. "But with hot girls like you, boyfriends have to be on their toes all the time. Otherwise, someone will manage to sneak you away, right under their noses."

They all laughed.

Janay put her hand on Fitz's arm. "Is that what happened with you and that girl...what was her name?"

"You mean, Christina?" He took a swig from his bottle. "No. She was just too busy with her work. Didn't want to step out and have some fun, barely free during weekends. And you know me. I crave time with other people. What I need is a girl who's like me."

Janay opened her mouth to say something but just then, Mason sauntered back to their table. He nudged her. "Hey, Janay, thanks! Kiera and I are taking off." He gestured for her to give him a high five. "I owe you one!"

"Good luck!" she whispered for only Mason to hear, "Be good to her or you'll have to answer to me."

Mason nodded with a smile and wound his way back out towards the door where Kiera waited.

Janay eyed them until they stepped out. A sweet feeling of euphoria spread through her heart. It felt nice to hook people together and give them the opportunity to discover the good things about each other. Of course, she wished she could do the same for herself. But whereas, her vision regarding others seemed clear and unhindered, she couldn't say the same thing when it came to her own love life. It'd been a while since she'd been in a long-term relationship. Men were plentiful and she never did without male attention for long, but she'd grown tired of it all. Maybe it had something to do with the fact that one of her sisters got married last year. The other one would be getting hitched this year. It definitely made her the odd one out in the family.

Not that it bothers me. I'm still young.

Well, all right, maybe it bothered her just a little bit. She felt like the odd wheel whenever she hung out with them. Perhaps it'd come time to pay more attention to her rather lonely life.

"Hey. Earth calling Janay!" Fitz tapped her bottle with his. "What happened?"

"Umm—nothing!" She forced a bright smile. She surveyed the people at the table. Who needed a man when she was surrounded by such amazing friends? She was indeed lucky to have these people in her life. She was free and full of fun...just the way she liked it.

CHRISTMAS CUPID

Chapter Two

With a surreptitious glance, Fitz feasted on Janay's glowing face...A woman after his own heart. He didn't know how long it'd been since he first craved her attention. In high school, it seemed like a mild crush. He never acted on it because he wasn't sure if she would take too kindly to him wanting to be more to her than just her socially-awkward-but-best-guy-friend. During law school, he dated several girls but somehow, it never materialized into anything strong and long lasting. When he moved back to New York and met Janay again, he finally discovered why every woman fell short of his expectations. He, Randy Fitzgerald, Fitz to no one but Janay, was the problem. He'd been in love with her for many years.

No woman could compare to her.

Sure she was beautiful and sexy, but he loved her feisty, take-charge, I'm-not-gonna-take-shit attitude just as much. Only her family and close friends knew that under her ballsy, tough-as-nails exterior lay a heart of gold. She was loyal and compassionate, too. He enjoyed spending time with her. Sometimes, he imagined running his fingers through her dark hair, touching her smooth, warm, dark skin, kissing and making long, sweet, hot love to her. Just thinking about it made him aroused. Fitz shook his head. The same thing as spinning castles in the air. If he didn't do something, someone would snatch her soon enough.

He wanted to ask her out on a real date and considered making the move on more than one occasion. What stopped him each time was the realization that if she wasn't interested, which she didn't seem to be, he would lose out on a great friend. He didn't want to risk that. Also, there hardly seemed to be a time when she wasn't super busy. She was, after all, the financial brain behind Riley's Grand Events, a business in which she co-owned with her sisters, Lexi and Brielle. Not to mention the fact that she was a popular girl and didn't lack for male attention. Situations like this were rare, in which they were both single at the moment. It would be the perfect time to take his chance...to make his move.

The problem was—she appeared so clueless about his feelings that he just didn't know how to spring this on her. She might dismiss him summarily and that would not only adversely affect their easy relationship, but it would break his heart. What made these circumstances more frustrating was the fact that *he knew* they were perfect for each other. They were interested in the same things, enjoyed similar activities, had a strong network of mutual friends and even shared the same core values. A pity really, that she couldn't see what existed right under her nose. Janay seemed to be good at matchmaking other couples, yet she failed to see him as the perfect man for her.

Without being egotistic, he knew that together, they would be a stick of dynamite. Explosive. But how could he convey that idea to her?

It would be best if she came to the realization on her own. It would make the biggest impact. Then when he asked her out, she wouldn't—hell, couldn't—say no. So, how could he turn the whole thing around, so it would be her who chased him, rather than the other way around?

"Now that Kiera and Mason seem to hit it off, who's next on your agenda?" Jason asked.

Jason's question jolted Fitz back to the present.

"I would ask her to find me a guy, but I'll take a rain check. I've been hopping from one relationship to another like some kind of relationship grasshopper and it's so not good for my emotional health," Sandra complained. "But I seem to be attracted to the wrong kind of guy, so it would be a relief to be on my own for a while."

Janay's lips lifted in a wicked smile. "Tell me when you're ready. I think I have someone in mind for you."

Sandra leaned closer. "Who's he?"

Janay tapped her fingers against her beer bottle. "Didn't you just say that you wanted to be alone for a while?"

"I did." Sandra bit her bottom lip as she considered Janay's words. "You're deliberately trying to tempt me. That's not fair."

Janay's tinkling laughter was full of mirth.

Fitz loved seeing that naughty gleam in her eyes. The girl was simply too enticing. He longed to pull her into his arms and deliver a kiss, but she would probably slap him, or worse, make it seem like a joke. With an effort, he kept his hands on the table.

"Let me know when you're ready." She chuckled. "Janay is my name and matchmaking is my game," she said in a singsong voice. "You'll be in good hands." She rubbed her palms together. "But you have to be ready to put yourself entirely in my hands."

Her words triggered an idea in his mind. Fitz refined it as he strolled to the bar to get another drink. When he returned, they were talking about another couple who were married and were soon to be parents. Janay took credit for their happy ending also. If only his silly woman could see how her happiness wasn't that far from her grasp.

If she ever got away from this crazy obsession of hers.

Then it hit him. He shaped the very idea rolling around in his head into a perfect plan to lure her exactly where he wanted her to be. "What about me?"

Janay turned to face him. "What?

He shrugged, enjoying her attention. "I'm single. You could set me up with someone."

She narrowed her eyes. "But you always said that you were perfectly capable of finding the right girl on your own."

"It's obvious that I haven't succeeded. Maybe I could benefit from your expert help. What do you think?"

She snorted. "You're pulling my leg."

"No, I'm not," he insisted, enjoying the befuddled expression on her face. Was she already feeling unease at the idea of hooking him up with someone? Perhaps she couldn't bear the thought of seeing him with another girl? "Are you up for the challenge?"

"Okay." She took a sip from her bottle as she eyed him. "Let's do this. You'll be my next project."

"I can hardly wait," he quipped in a dry voice.

Sandra raised an eyebrow at him.

Janay seemed to miss the irony in his tone.

"So, how shall we go about it?"

She eyed him with care. "Generally, I get this feeling, you know. I see a person and I can sense what they need. Strange, that I'm not getting it for you. It might help if you could tell me what kind of qualities you would like your woman to have?"

"Shouldn't you know that? I mean, you know me better than anyone else."

"That's true," she admitted. "Let me see...your woman should be easygoing, sensitive but not overly so. You would hate a crying, attention-seeking woman. An independent woman would attract you. She should be passionate about her work, life and friends. And of course, family should be important for her. Loyalty. Honesty. Commitment to family and friends. All these are good traits to have. And a sense of humor is a big plus."

"Is that all that he would like?" Sandra interjected sardonically. "And I thought it was only the women who were picky. How the hell are you going to find such a paragon of virtue?"

"She doesn't have to be perfect." Janay pointed to Fitz. "He certainly isn't." She appeared to be concentrating hard. "I can see him with a person who's talkative, fun and yet, practical. They should be friends first, lovers later. And the woman should also be able to sit with him through soccer games and enjoy going to bars and clubs on weekends."

Can't you see it? That perfect woman for me is you!

Of course, he couldn't say it out loud. Subtlety would be crucial. If she stumbled on this idea that they belonged together on her own, she would move heaven and earth to make sure they ended up together. He knew her...a downright determined girl.

"That's a long list. I can hardly see anyone fitting with all of these standards," Fitz added in an attempt to see if it sparked off something in her mind.

CHRISTMAS CUPID 19

She remained oblivious to his hints. "Your woman should also be well-read and knowledgeable. Otherwise, you'll get bored. And she shouldn't be clingy. Right?"

How could she be so dense? "You've hit the nail on the head."

Janay pumped her hand in the air. Excitement shone in her eyes. "I knew it. Now, all I've to do is find her."

Sandra, who sat listening to the whole conversation intently, snorted. "The perfect person for you would be—"

Fitz's glare cut off her words.

She spluttered, as if a light bulb suddenly lit inside her mind. Her mouth opened and closed. She glanced from him to Janay and then smiled. "I'm sure Janay will be able to find someone who can fit into your life."

"Oh! I've no doubt that she'll do her best. If anyone can do this, she can." He winked at Sandra, knowing she'd caught on to the idea. *Will she give the game away?*

Then her eyes narrowed in speculation while she gazed at Janay, who still seemed to be deep in thought as if she were mentally reviewing all the women she knew. "Best of luck, Janay," she said as she stood. "Listen, you guys, I better go. I've got a family thing tomorrow."

Janay waved her hand in an absent-minded gesture. "See you."

"Hey, Sandra. Is your brother still working in that construction company?" Fitz glanced at Janay. "Excuse us a minute. I just need to know something." He walked Sandra out. "Thanks for not spilling the beans."

She made no attempt to pretend she didn't know what he was talking about. "I had no idea you had a thing for her."

"For a long, long time," he admitted.

"I hope, for your sake, that it works out. But wouldn't it be easier to just tell her?"

"She would shoot me down like a pile of tins at the fair. We've been friends for too long."

Sandra sighed. She hailed a cab. "That's true. You're in her comfort zone."

"And that's why she would hate to plunge into something that could ruin our friendship." He scratched his cheek thoughtfully as he opened the cab door for her and assisted her inside. "Nothing with that woman is ever easy."

"Good luck. You two would be great together."

"Yeah, if only Janay could see that." He smiled. "Thanks, Sandra. See you."

She blew him a kiss goodbye.

When he sauntered back inside, Janay was talking to their other friends. "What did you want to talk her about?"

"Just needed some information on the construction industry," he lied smoothly. "Her brother would be a valuable source. So, have you thought of someone for me yet?"

Janay chuckled. "You've got to be patient, dude. What's the hurry? It's not magic, you know. A lot of hard work goes into it." She punched him lightly on the arm. "The rewards will be worth the effort I put into it. Trust me."

"I can't wait to start my life with someone, you know? It's a bitch being single." He gazed into her deep, dark eyes. Desire curled in the pit of his stomach. Why couldn't she see that he was crazy about her? Why couldn't she read the passion in his eyes and sense the deep longing in his heart? No one knew him better than she did. Yet...she was the one who failed to read his intentions.

It might just be a foolish plan. In fact, it did sound kind of crazy. But perhaps, everything would fall into place. He surely hoped so. If this failed, he didn't have a backup idea. It had to work, he convinced himself as he edged his way closer to her. If it didn't, he would just have to ask her out anyway. What could be the worst that would happen? She might say no. But at least, he would have given it his best shot.

Although, he hoped with all this effort, it would bring the results he sought.

Chapter Three

Janay picked up the files from her desk and dropped them into the drawer, but taking care to place one back in its exact position. Lexi, her sister, was a stickler for details. If she misplaced a single paper or file, she would get THE LECTURE. And yeah, she would rather avoid it.

As she closed the drawer, Lexi and Brielle sauntered in. "I'm not sure about white roses. I was thinking more about carnations," Brielle was speaking, "Maybe we need to rework the center pieces."

"We're not reworking anything," Lexi stated in a firm voice, then rolled her eyes. Holding Brielle's hand, she took a deep breath and exhaled. "Listen, I've planned this for more than a hundred brides. Trust me. Everything is under control. Your wedding will be amazing. All you need to do is to think about your dress and dream about your honeymoon. Janay and I will manage all the other details."

Brielle chewed at her bottom lip. "You're right. I'm sorry. There's no need to get worked up over small things. But I need to plan the menu for the wedding."

"You've trained John and he's going out of his way to plan a menu and serve food that will live up to the excellent reputation that you've earned with hard work. If you interfere, it will be an insult to his dedication and love."

Good job! Janay wordlessly applauded Lexi. Appealing to Brielle's kind and sensitive side was always the best way to get things done.

"Yes, you're right." Brielle took a chair. "I'm sorry. It's silly to be worrying over it all. And I'm giving you a hard time...while you're pregnant."

Lexi's smile lit the room. She took a seat and patted her stomach, looking glowingly happy. "It's your wedding. You're entitled to get nervous, but we'll manage things. And my pregnancy is progressing exactly as it should."

Janay reclined on her chair, glad for the excuse to take a break from her duties and have a little sibling-time with Lexi and Brielle. It was still hard for her to believe she was going to be an aunt soon. The happiness bubbling inside her was fierce and strong. She felt quite excited about this new arrival in their family. The bond she shared with her sisters was pure and powerful. She felt forever grateful that she not only had the opportunity to live near them, but also work with them. Sometimes, they had their ups and down, but it always got sorted out in time and without a lot of fuss. She loved them and they were fiercely protective of her. "What about your nausea?" she asked.

"I experience it a little bit in the morning, but it's nothing major. Cole is more worried about it than I am. He damn near hovers over me until I leave the house." A smile played on her lips as she talked about her husband. "And he's taking a personal interest in everything I eat. It's annoying."

"Quit complaining," Janay chided as she wrinkled her nose. "You're lucky to have such a doting husband. Cole is a sweetheart."

"True, true." Lexi sighed. "So, tell me about the Carter's wedding. Did they finally select a menu?"

Janay nervously shifted in her chair. She'd been hoping to avoid giving this news, but now there was no other way around it. "They called to cancel."

Lexi shot up. "Cancel? Why? What did they say?"

"Relax!" Janay stood, walked over and rested her hand on Lexi's shoulder. "You're pregnant, remember."

Lexi sat back down, but worry showed in her eyes. "How can I not be tense about it? This is the sixth cancellation this year. What's going on? It can't be a coincidence. Something's up. There have never been so many cancellations before." She reached for the phone on the desk. "Let me call them."

"No!" Janay ran a hand through her hair as she decided how much she needed to tell Lexi. She went back to her seat, scooted the chair back and sat.

Brielle put her hand on hers. "We've got to tell her."

Lexi leaned forward, looking determined. "What's going on? Are you guys hiding something from me?"

Brielle cleared her throat. "It's—Janay found out that Arianna has been spreading ugly rumors about us and our company to our clients and to whomever she comes into contact with."

"Arianna?" Lexi scowled. "Who the hell…?" Comprehension dawned slowly. "That Arianna? Cole's ex-fiancé? Didn't she get community service for what she did?" Lexi shook her head, her eyes pained. "She should've learnt her lesson."

"I guess she didn't." Janay put her hand on the table. "I've been talking to people who cancelled and they were all approached by her during some random events or in malls or in book clubs. She would accidently run into them and then bad-mouth us." Janay used air-quotes when she said the word *accidentally*.

"But how did she know that they're our clients?"

"She's still friends with people Cole knows. Some of her social circle is the same. Don't forget that her parents are loaded and she's a trust fund baby. She knows people. I've seen her in pubs and clubs and even at some events that we've hosted."

Lexi looked distressed. "And now, she has set out to destroy our business."

Anyone who put that look in her sister's eyes wasn't ever going to get away with it. Janay closed her hand into a fist. *Oh no! Arianna picked the wrong fight.* Janay wouldn't allow her to get away with it. All she needed to do was figure out how to hit that damn woman back and once she did, Arianna wouldn't stand a chance. "I don't want either of you to worry about this."

"Not worry?" Lexi's jaw dropped open. "This woman is systematically badmouthing us, trying to ruin the business we built from scratch and sacrifice and you're telling me—?"

Janay raised a hand, palm up. Resolve pumped through her. "I'm talking to the right people and getting a measure of this woman. She won't get away with it for long. Remember the Rogers who cancelled an event last year? One of my friends talked to them. They invited me up to their house and I explained the situation. They want to hire us for a party in January." She pumped her hand in the air. "So, one victory for us. Arianna won't get away with her lies. Soon, she'll be exposed and the truth will come out."

"But that won't stop her."

Janay nodded. "We would have to find a more permanent solution, but until then, I'm approaching all the old clients who cancelled and giving them a chance to reconsider their opinion about us."

"Maybe I should tell Cole to talk to her?" Lexi mused.

"Bad move!" Janay vetoed the idea. "Listen, I'm handling it. Let me come up with a plan. But if you have any ideas, we could work on them."

Lexi and Brielle stared at each other.

Janay drummed her fingers on the desk. "Great! So, we'll do it my way. Let me get some more information on this woman and then I'm going to devise a strategy that will blow her out like a candle. Once I'm done with her, she won't know what hit her. Give me some time."

Lexi sighed. "All right."

The sisters got to talking about the other weddings and events they were signed up for. Janay's cell phone dinged. Picking it up, she checked her message. A smile flitted across her lips.

"What is it?" Lexi didn't miss a trick. "Anyone we know?"

"Oh! It's just Fitz. I set him up on a date and he's sending me updates."

Brielle shifted to face her. "You set up Randy on a date? Don't tell me you've taken him on as one of your matchmaking projects?"

"Sort of, yes. He wanted me to do it." Her sisters never approved of her attempts to put people together as sometimes, it got her in front of the firing range. "And I've found the perfect girl for him. Met her in the salon. She's exactly the person he needs in his life."

Brielle ran her finger over the edge of the desk. "I like Randy. He's sweet, very caring and determined in his career goals. In fact..." She shook her head. "Whoever he ends up with will be a lucky girl."

"Back to our work." Lexi's voice sounded clipped. "We're still running a business."

So, they shifted the discussion to various projects that they had on the upcoming schedule.

After the meeting came to an end, Janay checked over the accounts for the last month. Finishing and filing them, she went into the preparation area to take inventory of all the stuff they brought over from their warehouse for the next day's event. Although she was the financial head of the company, she was often delegated to do other work. Since it was a business owned and run by the three sisters, they were involved in all aspects of it. Luckily, they didn't have an event tonight. Around five o'clock, she strode out. Fitz asked her to meet at a café for coffee, so they could rehash his date.

Yeah! She could tell she was on to something. The woman she set him up with was a nice person. He would be sure to like her. Excitement frizzled inside her. She felt immensely proud of her matchmaking abilities. She gleaned a certain level of satisfaction when couples ended up together because of her efforts. Also, Fitz had been alone for a long time. It would be interesting to put him together with someone who made him happy. While she marched along the busy roads, she imagined Fitz with a woman who matched him on all levels. Sharon, the girl she set him up with, was perfect in a lot of ways. Of course, Janay didn't know her as well as her older friends, but she did have a sweet disposition. She seemed to enjoy going out and meeting new people...quite a fun girl to be around.

She tried to imagine them together.

A hot lance of pain exploded inside her stomach as she visualized Fitz with Sharon. It was such an unexpected powerful feeling that for a moment, she halted, unable to process the reason for it. Why would she feel so murderous at the thought of Fitz being with someone else? She saw him plenty of times with other women. Why couldn't he be with Sharon?

Or maybe she didn't like the idea of him being with any woman.

Was that it?

Realizing she'd just stopped in the middle of the sidewalk and people were brushing past her, she began to walk again.

Did she feel jealous? For god's sake, why?

Fitz was her friend. She wanted him to find his bliss with another soul. Why would she feel anxious or unhappy about it? It seemed totally stupid to think like this. Flabbergasted by this new feeling, she fought to dismiss the thought from her mind as she reached the café.

Fitz waited in a corner booth. When he spotted her, he waved.

With a light smile, she joined him. "Hi. So, how was it? Give me all the juicy details." She eyed the waiter who was heading their way. She felt impressed with his efficiency.

"Impatient, aren't you?" Fitz replied. "What will you have?"

"Café latte and one of their caramel cookies."

Fitz then placed his order. "All right, in summary, it was nice," he said when the waiter moved out of earshot.

"Nice?" Janay wrinkled her nose. "That's not the way you're supposed to describe a dynamite date."

"It wasn't dynamite."

"Oh, oh! What went wrong?" Even though she pulled a long face, Janay became aware of how little pings of relief were zooming inside her. It seemed like such a strange reaction that she couldn't make heads or tails of it. Why would she be relieved if his date didn't work out? "Sharon is a great girl."

"Yes, She is. But you know...that spark was missing."

"You're a tough cookie," she mused.

The waiter brought her coffee and cookies.

Picking up the pale brown, round delicacy, she bit into it. "You present a hard challenge, my friend. But don't you worry; I'm up for it. I'll find the perfect girl for you soon enough."

His gaze bored into hers. "I'm sure you will. Anyway, so let me tell you what happened."

While he launched into a long description of his date, her thoughts wandered to other matters. Why was this matchmaking effort different than the others? Before, she always felt excited to get great results, but here, in Fitz's case, she actually felt happy Sharon wasn't the one for him. Probably because she didn't take her time to select the right person. On an instinctive level, she must've known he wouldn't hit it off with Sharon.

It would be all right. She just needed to keep looking.

Sooner or later, she would find the one girl who made him happy. Of course, she would have to be pretty amazing. The woman in his life needed to have a lot of good qualities because he was more than a special guy. He deserved the best. She took the last few sips of her coffee. "I should go." She stood. "Don't fret. I'm going to find someone else for you."

"Let me walk you home."

"No need," she said breezily as she took out her wallet to pay for her share. "My apartment is right around the corner."

He waved down her efforts to pay for her part of the bill. "Come on. Let's go."

When he insisted on going with her, she didn't protest too much. Truth be told—she enjoyed Fitz's company. Most days, they didn't get a chance to spend much time together, but now with this new matchmaking project she'd taken on, it would be a good opportunity for them to hang out some more. Janay bounced along, her step light and happy. "How's work coming along?"

"Good. In fact, my boss is so happy that he has pretty much promised me a generous bonus this year. I've been thinking of a holiday destination. You know, like somewhere I can relax and enjoy on a beach for two weeks."

"Hawaii!" she offered.

"Nah! I was thinking somewhere more exotic. Thailand?"

"I've never been there."

"Well, why don't you..." He paused. "...Yeah! That sounds like a good place. I'll check it out on the internet. Imagine; me, beach, sun, sand and a cool drink. It'll be a slice of heaven."

She could very well visualize what he described. More than that, she could imagine being with him in such a beautiful place. When the image popped into her head, she ran a hand through her hair, unsure about what was happening. Why would she be with Fitz on a vacation? Of course, they could go as friends. It would be silly, wouldn't it? Especially, when she was busy setting him up with another girl!

Maybe she needed a break and that's why she was having such silly fantasies. What with all the tension regarding the hellcat who kept trying to destroy their reputation and planning Brielle's wedding, she was too tense.

That has to be it!

"It sounds delightful," she managed to say without giving him an indication of the storm brewing inside of her. "When do you plan to go?"

"Not for another four or five months. There's an interesting project I'm working on and if it finishes as I hope, I'll be able to enjoy the vacation even more." He smiled. "How are the preparations coming along for Brielle's wedding?"

"She's going nuts, like all brides do. But of course, Lexi and I are there to calm her down. Lexi's pregnant."

"Hey! That's great news." He put an arm around her shoulder and gave her a tight hug.

A strange, jolting feeling skidded along her nerves at the brief touch. She liked the way her body bumped against his.

"You're going to be an aunt soon. I'm sure everyone's excited."

His hand on her shoulder practically burned. She wanted to pull away to stop the electric current zinging up and down her arm at the brief touch. And yet, she didn't. What the hell is wrong with her? This is Fitz. There must have been a million times when he touched her like this before. *What is so different about this brief contact today?* "Yes, we all are."

"Here we are." He halted as he glanced up at the three-storied building that housed her place. All three sisters shared it. Each one of them had her own apartment, a gift from their parents. This ensured that they not only stayed together, but were able to support each other in times of need. "I guess I'll see you." Bending his head, he deposited a light kiss on her lips.

It felt like the barest touch of his lips to hers and yet, her insides turned to jelly. "Bye."

When he strolled away, she stood rooted to the spot. Her lips were fairly ablaze. Just a light kiss, even a chaste one. An almost brotherly kiss. A sensation curled in her veins and swept through her and it wasn't platonic at all. In fact, she had sizzled with the need to pull him back and kiss him good and proper. She wanted to run her fingers through his thick, black hair that reminded her so much of blackberries, slip her arms around his neck and press her body into his.

Damn it! There is definitely something wrong with her mind. Surely, she imagined the attraction she felt towards him.

It couldn't be real!

It simply couldn't be!

This was Fitz! Her best friend! Her pillar of support! She couldn't be harboring such feelings for him. Janay sighed as she walked into the building. Maybe it was time to take a hot bath and rid her mind of these useless thoughts and feelings. Something was seriously wrong with her. Perhaps it's just the stress of work and the excitement of a wedding in the family and the arrival of a new life. Surely, she would be able to return to her normal state of mind soon.

Yes! That's it, or is it something else?

Chapter Four

After yet another unsuccessful date, Fitz was rethinking his not-so-brilliant idea. Instead of falling in with his plans, Janay acted even more gung-ho about the whole process. Every day, she appeared eager to suggest the names of women he would be deliriously happy with. Why couldn't she see that he dreamt up this whole project only because he wanted her to realize she was perfect for him?

Maybe this wasn't such a good idea.

Or perhaps, it needed a little...amendment. He intended to work on it until it yielded results. In the evening, he stopped at her apartment.

Focus, Fitz, focus!

She opened the door. "Hey! What's up?"

"The last date was a disaster."

"Oh, no! Come in! Why?"

"She hates animals. Hates them with a passion! As in, she can't be in the same room with them. You know, I've always had pets. How am I supposed to be with a woman who's like that?"

She slapped a hand on her forehead. "I forgot to ask her about pets. Shit! I'm sorry, Fitz."

"It's all right." He took a seat at the kitchen table. "I've got a plan now."

"What plan?"

Fitz pressed his fingers hard against his thighs. He sure hoped this worked. "It's obvious you don't know me as well as we thought you did."

"I know you pretty well, Fitz," she argued.

When his name rolled off her tongue, he felt the desire to drag her into his arm. He cleared his throat. "Maybe we should spend some more time together, so you can get a feel of what makes me tick. Then, just maybe, you might be able to think of someone who's a good fit for me." He'd been the *safe, dependable Fitz* in her life for too long. It was time to become the-man-*she-had-the-hots-for Fitz*. He wanted her to crave him the same way he craved her. "You missed an important detail, Janay. I mean...pets? How could you forget that?"

She gave a dismissive wave of her hand. "Don't sweat the small stuff. Geez, it was a small mistake. I didn't forget Tiger. It just slipped my mind to check with her to see if she was okay with dogs, cats, that kinda thing."

"And that's why it's important for us to spend more time with each other, so you're on top of things." He frowned for good measure. "I thought you were serious about this?" He threw the challenge out lightly, deliberately.

As expected, she drew herself to her full 5 feet 6 inches. "Of course, I am."

"If you aren't..." He stood, firmly keeping a check on his lips that itched to smile. It wasn't difficult to rile her...Push a few buttons and she would agree to whatever he said.

"I said I am, didn't I?" she huffed. "I'm free right now. Let's sit and talk."

He raised his brows. "That would be too contrived, don't you think?"

"Oh! You're impossible. Give me a minute. We'll change and go grab a cup of coffee or something." She walked out without waiting for a response. "Men!" she muttered.

Fitz resisted the urge to do a victory dance. He waited with a calm exterior until she came back and picked up her purse from the couch. "Actually, I've got a better idea."

"What is it?" Suspicion coated her words.

"Don't look at me as if I'm going to ask you to battle a pride of lions with me." He stood. "Come on."

"Tell me where we're going, Fitz," she griped as they went out of the apartment. She locked her door. "Is it a restaurant?"

He knew she didn't like surprises. However, he enjoyed keeping her a little off balance. She was so sharp and bright, he seldom got the chance to do it. "Patience, my lovely!"

When they went down the stairs, they saw Lexi and Cole.

Cole kept struggling to take two bags of groceries from Lexi's hands while he carried four already. "Let go," he ordered.

Lexi sniffed. "I'm perfectly capable of carrying them up the stairs. I'm not taking the elevator." She gazed down at her belly that hadn't started to show signs of her condition as yet. "Pregnancy doesn't make me an invalid, Cole."

"The doctor said—"

"He didn't say anything about not being able to carry stuff," she snarled.

Fitz took the packets away from Lexi before she realized what he was up to. "How are you doing?" He kissed her on the cheek. "Congratulations! I heard the good news."

She raised an eyebrow, glanced down at the grocery bags that were now in his hands and rolled her eyes. "Not you, too! Fine. I'm okay. Doing well. And I'm due in July."

"An Independence baby!" He beamed.

"She's fine, but I'm having a tough time with the mood swings," Cole whispered and sighed.

"I heard that, Cole," Lexi retorted. She jammed her now empty hands against her hips.

Cole continued as if he hadn't heard her, "The doctor assured me that she should be through this phase in a couple of months." He sighed again. "I can't wait to get my Lexi back."

"Cole!" Lexi thundered.

Cole, Janay and Fitz exchanged amused glances.

Fitz gestured to the packages he'd confiscated from Lexi. "Let me just drop these upstairs and I'll be right back." He took the stairs, two at a time.

The group waited until he came back down, then Cole used the respite to press the control of the elevator. By the time Lexi figured what he'd done, the doors of the elevator swished opened. Cole took the elbow of the bemused Lexi and escorted her inside.

They both watched in amusement as the couple disappeared from view when the doors closed with a firm snap.

Janay laughed and turned to Fitz. "Nicely done!" She applauded as they stepped away. "She's just struggling with nausea these days but she tries to hide it."

"The original tough lady, she is."

She tucked her hand under his arm. "So, where are we going?"

"Wait and see!" They strolled out and along on the sidewalk. This was perfect. He could spend an entire lifetime walking around with her. "So, any new guy in your life?"

"Nope! Not even looking right now. I liked Sandra's theory and am taking a similar break from men."

Fitz breathed a sigh of relief. *Good! Great news, actually.* He didn't want to fight off another man while he made a play for

CHRISTMAS CUPID 39

her. They walked along for another twenty minutes until finally he saw the sign. "There! We're going to that fun fair."

"Fun fair! Have you lost your mind?" She tried to yank her hand out of his grip. "It's for kids."

"We've been to plenty of fun fairs before."

"Yeah, when we were twelve and way too long ago."

He tugged her forward. "And that's why this is the perfect time to go."

"I'm too old for this kind of thing."

"No, you're not. And neither am I." He bought the tickets. "Come on. If you don't have fun, we'll get out whenever you say the word."

She glowered at him.

He wriggled his eyebrows at her.

"Fine," she huffed as they went inside.

Fitz surveyed the brightly lit stalls and the noisy crowds milling about. Children chased each other through the throngs of people.

"This is crazy. What are we going to do here?" she asked

He pointed to a stall with large, stuffed animals. "Let's do that. I'll win you a prize."

"Please! You're a lousy shot." Raising a hand, she mimed shooting. "And I was the one who won you a prize last time."

He grimaced. "Oh, yeah...When we were twelve. I've been taking shooting lessons for the past two years."

Her mouth gaped open. "You have? I didn't know that."

"See! There's already one more thing you now know that you didn't before. Admit it, my plan is working already."

She rolled her eyes. "All right, fine. Do you want me to say it? Yes, Fitz, this was a great idea. Now, tell me why you've been taking shooting lessons?"

"A friend of mine got me into it. It's a great way to release my frustration."

"You're never frustrated."

Little did she know! Her presence already tied him in knots. It felt like torture to be with her and not be able to kiss or touch her. But he couldn't tell her that. Of course, not. But soon, yeah! He would get her to where he wanted her. He paid the money and picked up the gun. "That's not true. I get frustrated by some things, such as women who think I can't even win a damned prize."

She slapped him on the arm. "Show me your skills, big man!"

Oh, how he longed to show her. But for now, this would have to suffice. He took careful aim and shot straight on the dot. A few minutes later, he held a periwinkle-blue teddy bear in his hands. He presented it to her with a flourish. "For you, my lady."

She accepted with a giggle. "Thank you."

"I'll carry it for you," he offered. "You want to go on the Ferris wheel?"

"I hate it." She pulled a face. "Let's do the pirate ship first. It's my favorite."

He hated the pirate ship but didn't say anything as she bounced towards the ride. If it made her happy, he would walk on hot coals. This was nothing. As expected, the ride was horrible. He fought the urge to throw up.

"Are you all right?" she asked when they got down from it.

Bile rose in his throat. With an effort, he swallowed and nodded. "Never better."

"Note to self; Fitz doesn't like pirate ships." She laughed. "This was a brilliant idea. I'm getting to know so much about you."

This wasn't what he had in mind. He expected to make an impression, but instead, he came across as a wimp. The roller coaster came next. Now—he actually thought he would throw up. But much to his relief, he didn't. Later, he treated her to a hot dog.

"Having fun?"

She held his hand as they walked towards another stand. "Thank you. I'm having a lovely time."

Her brief touch sent a shiver of delight up along his spine. He controlled the emotions swirling inside him. Seeing her laughing, happy face right next to him, he wanted to pull her into his arms and crush his mouth over hers. Yeah, that would totally throw her off. He couldn't afford to give up the game so quickly. She still didn't realize what he was doing. Maybe it would be a good idea to keep it like that for a little while. "So, what about tomorrow?"

She stopped to buy cookies and ice cream. "What do you mean?"

"You agreed that this was a good idea. I think we should do this again."

She offered him a cone.

He shook his head.

"Fun fair again?"

"Nope!" He considered the options. Together, they did a lot of interesting things: theatre, cinema, restaurants and even hiking. This time though, he wanted to take her out of the comfort zone and do something different. It was important to let her see he wasn't the same old friend with whom she felt comfortable. Instead, he needed her to see him in a new light. "How about ice skating?"

She cringed. "What? I'll break a bone or something."

"Don't worry. I'll help you."

Her eyes narrowed in suspicion. "Did you take skating lessons, too?"

"Yeah! Three years ago. A bunch of us used to go for ice skating regularly, and then they moved out of town and I just never found a partner who enjoyed it as much I did. So, I don't usually go now. But it would be great to teach you. How can you live in New York and never go ice skating?"

She thought for a minute, a contemplative look in her eyes.

Fitz could almost see the wheels whirring in her mind.

"Sounds like a plan."

While he walked her back to the apartment, happiness bubbled deep inside him. His plan appeared to be working. He surely hoped so, because without it, he didn't have anything else to fall back on. And he couldn't stomach the idea of losing her to another man.

CHRISTMAS CUPID

Chapter Five

A week later, Janay rang the bell to Fitz's apartment. In her hands, she held Chinese takeout, his favorite. Of course, she should've called first, or maybe sent a text. What if he wasn't home? She was an idiot. He did have a date for lunch today. Maybe he's still with the girl even now. What if they were in the apartment, doing—?

Her imagination went into overdrive as she saw flashes of them wrapped in each other's arms. A sharp pain stabbed her heart.

What the hell is that?

Nothing, she assured herself. It's nothing. Lately, she and Fitz were spending so much time together that it was hard to imagine him with another girl. She wasn't jealous, certainly not. Why would she be? And yet, a hot and fiery ball of emotion burned in her stomach. Taken aback by the unfamiliar feelings of jealousy and resentment, she remained rooted to the spot even though he opened the door.

"Hey! What are you doing here? Come in." When she didn't move, he frowned. "Janay? Are you all right?"

The concern in his voice galvanized her into action. She forced a smile. "Yes, of course. I brought food. Maybe you're busy, I should've called before. I could just leave—it's okay."

"Relax, Janay. I wasn't doing anything." He closed the door behind her and took the bags from her hands. "Smells good. And you got it at Mi Kow; smart move."

"Yeah, I know that you've got a standing order over there." She chuckled. "I just told them to give me double of whatever you usually take."

"Good decision." He put the bags of food on the kitchen counter. "I was thinking about catching a movie. Relax a little, since it's back to the grind tomorrow."

"We could watch a movie after dinner," she suggested. Embarrassment pooled in her heart. *Down, girl!* What the hell was wrong with her? Why was she assuming he would like to spend time with her? But then again, she'd never felt nervous around Fitz before. In fact, she took him pretty much for granted. Always just there. Her friend. Her support. Now today, she couldn't seem to get a grip on the flood of unfamiliar emotions pulsing through her. "That is, if you didn't have plans with anyone else."

"No. I would love that. Action, fantasy, or your favorite, RomCom?"

Automatically, she opened his cabinets to take out plates and cutlery. She'd spent enough time in his place to know where everything was kept. "What?"

"Those are the only three choices available tonight. I checked on the net."

"Yeah, sure. Anything's fine."

"That's one of the things I like about you. Game for anything, aren't you?"

Is that all he liked about her? Did she inadvertently corner herself into the space reserved for old, easygoing friends who were available for good times, but never recalled for bigger, more important things? It never bothered her before. Now, it pricked her to realize he might look at her as just a friend, sort of an androgynous person, who was just there all the time.

She was a woman, for God's sake. Didn't he see that?

She halted—why the hell did she care if he noticed her in that light? They weren't dating. She'd never been interested in him in *that* way. No way! This was Fitz, her best friend. How could she even contemplate these things about him?

He tapped her on the shoulder.

She jumped. "What?"

"Are you okay? You've been standing in that spot with the plates in your hand for two minutes."

She wished the floor would open up and swallow her. Walking over briskly to the table where he already placed the food, she set the plates down. "Sorry. My mind is elsewhere." Of course, it was. She wanted to know more about his date—the reason for her unexpected arrival at his doorstop. Sure, she could've called and gotten details, but she didn't want to make it seem as if she cared very deeply about what he did with the woman. She was simply interested to know if he hit it off with her. After all, she did set them up. Maria was a good choice. Janay met her a year ago in a pub and they stayed in touch. She was nice and adored her three cats. They were a good match.

"So, what's going on? Met a new guy?" His voice sounded a little too chirpy.

"No! Told you I was off men for a while. Too much going on in our lives anyway. Brielle's wedding and Lexi's pregnancy. Between them, I'm going crazy. One of them is always deeply anxious about one thing or another. Thank god for Cole and

Toby. They're amazing. If they weren't there to handle the hissy fits and temper tantrums, I would've gone bonkers."

Fitz laughed as he took a seat. "It can't be easy to plan a wedding and prepare for the arrival of a new baby."

"Yeah. I want to buy something awesome for Lexi's baby shower. Brielle and I are planning it. But it's a surprise for Lexi."

He opened the boxes of food and served her.

Janay barely paid attention to the food. *God! Did he always looked this handsome? Or sexy?* Did his eyes always observe her with such intensity? Or, was she simply projecting her own feelings onto him?

"What are you planning to buy for the baby?"

"Haven't decided yet."

"There's this great shop called Trendy Babies. I could take you there. Went there with my friend the other day, because he wanted to buy a gift for his sister's child," he offered.

Her fork halted in mid-air. He's such a sweet guy. *Not going there, though!* Why was she thinking along these lines? She nodded. "Sure, that would be great. Or you could just give me the address—"

"No! I want to buy something for the baby too. So, what else have you been up to?"

There was a time when she could talk to him for hours. A few weeks ago, if he asked the same question, she would have regaled him with stories about her work or friends, or maybe they would've debated the last movie they saw or a book they both read. But today, her mind went absolutely blank. For the life of her, she couldn't think of something suitable to talk about. Everything seemed too childish, corny or silly.

Maybe she was coming down with something. She sure wasn't like this with him ever before. "Uh—it's just work, work and work. Christmas is a busy season."

"Are you guys still doing that pre-Christmas party at the senior citizens' home?"

"Yep. But this time, we'll do it at a different venue and we've organized a concert for them. We wanted to do something more classy and different. It's a small thing really. One of their favorite musicians has agreed to give a performance as a Christmas gift."

"Getting everyone to the venue would be difficult, right?"

"Yeah! Cole and Toby are pitching in and the house staff will also go. We've hired a bus for them all to transport back and forth from the location."

"I could come, too. Help you guys."

Once again, her fork halted on its way to her mouth. "Yeah, sure, that would be great." With an effort, she kept her tone light. "But don't you usually go for a company event or something?"

"They start late. I could finish with you guys, and then drop by over there. Maybe you could come with me. It would be nice to take a hot date with me for a change. I usually turn up alone."

Hot date? Does he really think so? Date? With him?

Fear and apprehension knotted in her stomach and exploded. What was he talking about? Did he actually mean it as a proper date? Or was it just a casual invitation? And what did he mean when he said she was hot? Once more, she became aware that a few weeks ago, she wouldn't have given his off-hand comment another thought. As friends, they went with each other on various events many times before.

Something surely had shifted in their relationship. Janay cleared her throat, then shoved a forkful of sweet and sour pork into her mouth.

Silence reigned in the room for a while as they both enjoyed the food. In contrast to her, Fitz seemed more at ease.

"How was your date?" She finally thought it was safe to enquire about the real reason she came here. "Maria is a great girl."

"Yeah! She's a nice person. We hit it off."

"You did?" Her pork almost got stuck in her throat. She wanted to punch Maria. "Really?"

"It's too early to say for sure." He ate with gusto, his face animated with emotion as he discussed it. "But we walked around a bit in Central Park. She enjoys quite a few things that I do. And we both love animals. In fact, she volunteers at an animal shelter."

"She's a real kind soul." If Maria was here, Janay might have picked up something and banged her on the head. *Why does she have to be so nice? And why the hell am I stupid enough to set up Fitz with the most amazing girl in the city*? Now, she would never see him. As a friend, of course. Naturally, the reason for the sour feeling now congealing in her stomach. It wasn't jealousy or some other totally inappropriate emotion. She felt happy that he liked this Maria.

Wasn't that the whole purpose of this exercise? She wanted him to end up with someone she admired and got along with. Maria was the right girl. She'd known it in her gut when she first thought of her. Then why did she suddenly feel as if her whole world just collapsed around her? She should be excited.

Instead, she felt devastated, broken.

If she didn't feel the excitement, she could fake it. "That sounds great. Told you, I'm an expert in matters of the heart."

"You're the best."

"So, did you guys set up another date?"

He waved his fork in the air. "I'm thinking about it. Didn't want to sound too eager. Although I am, if you know what I mean." He winked.

She felt a sudden urge to punch him on the nose.

"But I'm going to wait for a few days."

"Men!" she snorted. "Why do you feel that by keeping a woman hanging, you'll increase your chances with her?"

"I take it that you think I should call her now?"

"Umm..." Talk about bringing the axe down on her own foot. "Do whatever you think is best." She sniffed. Picking up her plate, she carried it over to the sink. While she rinsed it, Janay tried to marshal her thoughts and bring her emotions under check. This was unchartered territory. Having never felt such intense emotions for a friend before, she became very conscious of something going on inside her heart and mind that she couldn't make sense of. She was wrong to feel jealous of Fitz's new found happiness.

She wanted him to find his slice of joy. He deserved it because he was sweet and kind. Any woman would be lucky to have him. Not only was he good-looking and witty, but he was also great fun to be around. He would support his woman in times of need. He knew how to communicate, give and share...a rarity in most men.

If he's so perfect, why don't you snap him up yourself? A voice spoke inside her. She crushed it with a violent shake of her head. Just because she liked and admired Fitz didn't mean she felt attracted to him. It's just that they'd been friends for so long, it was difficult for her to let go and allow him to be with another woman who could fulfill his needs. He wouldn't stay single forever. Also, it was a good thing she was the one setting him up. It would ensure that she'd be able to remain friends with him even after he got married to Maria.

Married? Her heart slammed against her chest. They just went on one date, for crying out loud! Why was she hearing wedding bells? Even if she did, why did the thought bother her so much? Maybe it was time to reevaluate her feelings for Fitz. Her emotions were way out of line. While she should've been glad things were working out for him, what she really felt was the total opposite. Not only did she feel a super nasty twinge of jealousy, but she also felt angry with Fitz for actually liking the woman.

Talk about being irrational! She was certainly that at the moment.

It would better if she got a grip on her thoughts *before* she managed to ruin a beautiful friendship. Whatever the personal cost to her sanity, she wasn't willing to let go of Fitz. They'd always been friends—and they would remain so forever.

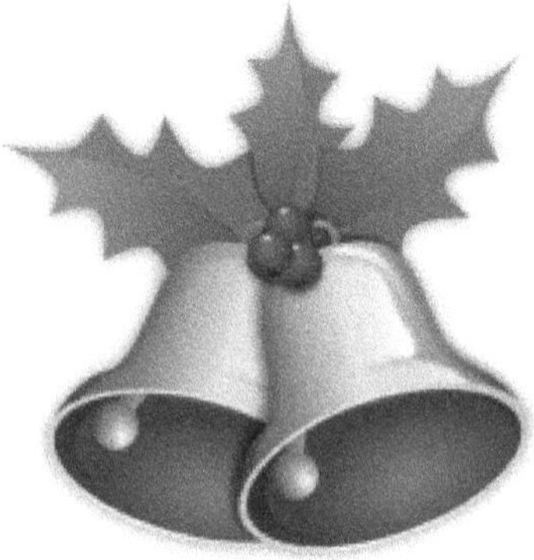

Chapter Six

His grand plan really seemed to be working. Fitz could sense her growing discomfort with the situation. When she turned up at his house to casually grill him about his date, it was a dead giveaway. She was getting antsy. Then, his decision to embellish his attraction to Maria was pure genius. He grinned as he logged out of his computer at the office. It was barely six in the evening. He could put in a little more work, but maybe it would be a good idea to drop by Janay's apartment and see how she was doing. Perhaps, he could discuss his plans with her to take Maria out for another date.

He wanted to rile her up.

Yet, he hated lying to her. If only she made things easy! Why couldn't she see how he was madly, stupidly in love with her? Everything she did charmed him. She was sexy, intelligent, kind and compassionate. There was nothing about her that he didn't like.

If he had his way, they would be wrapped in each other's arms right now.

However, Janay wasn't easy to get. He would have to line this up just right, if he wanted to land her. While he strode out of the building, his cell phone rang.

"Mr. Randy Fitzgerald?"

"Yes?" The voice sounded unfamiliar.

"I'm calling from the Medical Associates. Your mother was brought here after she collapsed at home and suffered a heart attack."

Fear and shock blanked his mind. "What?"

"She has been taken to the emergency. We would like you to come in, if possible."

Blood rushed to his head. He couldn't think, couldn't breathe. What was he supposed to do? With an effort, Fitz moved. He hailed a cab and barely waited for it to skid to a stop before he jumped in. "Medical Associates, please!" While the car drove off, he sent a text to Janay to inform her about what was happening. He tried to think of who else he should call, but his mind drew blank. When he reached the hospital, he paid the cabbie and rushed in. After getting details from the doctor on duty, he rushed to the emergency unit, but he wasn't allowed to see his mother. At least, not yet.

Fitz sat outside, not sure what he was supposed to do. His sister lived in Montana. He called her, relayed the news and pacified her as best as he could. When he shoved his smart phone back into his pocket, Janay strode in.

"Hey! How are you doing?" She bent to kiss his cheek and then sat next to him. "I checked my phone right before leaving the house and came straight here."

"I'm sorry to bother you," he said.

"Don't be silly." She squeezed his hand. "How is she doing?"

"They won't allow me to see—her." His voice broke a little. "But she's stable and needs to be monitored. If there isn't another attack within the next 24 hours—she'll be out of danger."

"You mom is going to make it, Fitz. You know how strong she is."

"I should've kept in touch with her more."

"You call her every day."

"I should've gone to see her. She never tells me when she isn't feeling well." He sighed, feeling the weight of guilt pressing down on his heart. "Luckily, the housekeeper was home and saw when she fell. If she hadn't been there..." Tears pricked at his eyes. "...She always goes home at five."

Janay rubbed a hand on his arm. "And when she's discharged from here, you'll insist that she hire a twenty-four assistant. She can't live alone."

Could he have done something different to avoid this situation? His mom was a healthy person. She hardly ever got sick. Who would've expected a heart attack? "Yeah, you're right. It's just..." He couldn't utter the words. What if something happened? He wasn't prepared to lose his mother. Their father died when Fitz was five and his sister was seven. Their mother raised them all alone. She'd been his support, his mentor, his friend. He wanted her in his life.

Janay gripped his hand in hers. "Nothing is going to happen to her. She'll be fine."

He took comfort in her words and in her presence. Together, they sat outside for a long time. The doctor came in to chat. "Mr. Fitzgerald, you can go home. We'll update you if there's any change."

He couldn't leave her. What if something happened after he left? Somehow, he felt his presence was important. She may not know it or sense it, but he needed to be here, close to her, if she needed him. "I'll wait here."

"We have a comfortable waiting area. You can take a seat there. I'll inform the nurse to contact you there if the need arises."

"Thank you." Fitz stood. "Janay, you should go home. It's late and there's no point in wasting your time."

"It's my time. I'll decide what to do with it." She gripped his arm and walked with him to the waiting area.

"You have work tomorrow?"

"Don't worry about that," she replied in a firm voice.

"I—"

"We should get some food," she cut off whatever protest he intended to make.

Knowing that nothing would make her change her mind, he stopped. Truth be told—he needed her presence. With her, he felt stronger and more capable of handling the situation. They ate dinner in the hospital cafeteria. Fitz could barely eat, but he forced himself to act normal. "The food wasn't as bad as I thought it would be," he said after they came up to the waiting room. "I mean, the pudding was actually sweet."

She laughed. "Yeah, you're right. Do you want coffee? I think I saw a machine outside."

"I'll get it."

"No, let me. I also need to call my sisters and update them."

A little while later she came in, carrying two steaming cups of coffee. They sipped coffee, watched the news on the TV, while they kept an ear turned towards the door, just in case a doctor came in.

Around two, Janay passed out on the couch.

He watched her face. Sleeping, she looked even more beautiful. Had he been thinking that he *liked* her? The word certainly wasn't enough to describe what he felt. He loved her, plain and simple. She'd been his anchor, not only in this time of need, but also in life. Without her, he would be lost. Suddenly, his mission to make her realize that they were perfect for each other seemed all the more important. If she didn't acquiesce to his way of thinking, his heart would break. This wasn't just a matter of dating her, although of course, he wanted to do that. But already, he was grappling with the thought of something more solid and permanent.

Lost in his thoughts and worried about his mother, Fitz finally managed to grab a few hours of sleep.

In the morning, he woke up when he felt a hand on his shoulder. "What?" He jumped up, disoriented and confused. Reality struck when his gaze took in the white coat of the doctor and the somber expression on his face. "Is she...?" He couldn't complete the sentence.

"Elena is doing much better than expected." The doctor grinned, not realizing how close he came to giving Fitz a heart attack. "In fact, you're allowed to see her for a few minutes."

"Thank you." Fitz gazed at Janay.

She stared at the two of them. Tears ran down her cheeks. She looked as delighted as he felt. "Go, go, go!" she chanted with a breathless cheer.

"No. You come with me." He grabbed her hand and tugged.

"But..." Janay turned towards the doctor.

"You can both go, but only for five minutes. We don't want to exert her."

They both rushed out to visit her.

His graceful, elegant mother looked miserable in the hospital bed. She wore a green hospital gown while looking frail. "Hey..."

"You gave me a scare," he complained as he leaned over to kiss her. But seeing her, happiness bubbled in his chest. She was alive and doing well. "Don't do it ever again."

A smile lifted her lips. "I'll try not to do it again. She glanced at Janay. "Hey, dear. Don't tell me you also stayed the night."

"We're just glad that you're doing well." Janay kissed her on the cheek. Not only did she know his mother since she was a kid, but she was very fond of the older woman. "And now you need to get out of the hospital as quickly as possible."

"Sure, will."

The nurse hovered over them.

Janay signaled to Fitz.

He kissed his mother and promised to visit in the evening if the doctor allowed. They stepped out. Fitz felt a lot more relieved than before.

"Let's go have breakfast," Janay suggested.

"Yeah." Fitz followed her out. They hailed a cab. "We could go to my place."

She raised an eyebrow. "Hmm...I'm afraid my selection of breakfast would be a lot better."

"All right, but you're cooking."

"Typical male!" She closed her eyes and leaned back. "It was a close call, wasn't it?"

"Yeah, it was." Love welled in his heart for the woman who could feel his pain almost as acutely as he did. He also knew her bond with his mother was strong too. No other woman would have stayed the night with him in the hospital. Janay was the one. Now, more than ever, he felt sure of it.

If she thought she would get away from him, she had another thought coming. He would chase her to the end of the world if it would mean making her his. His to hold. His to protect. His to love.

When they reached her apartment, he paid the cabbie.

After they stepped into her apartment, she headed for the bathroom. "Just give me a few minutes and then I'll start breakfast."

"I'll start the ball rolling." All night long, he didn't feel hungry but suddenly, he was famished.

By the time she came out after a quick shower, he'd made the batter for the pancakes.

"That was fast. I thought I was the one doing the cooking."

"I like to surprise you." He grinned. "Hand me the pan, *Madame*," he said with a mock flourish.

While he made pancakes, she set up some fruit and coffee on the kitchen table and they had a nice breakfast together. They ate quickly, in companionable silence. There wasn't much to say. People who stuck together through difficult times didn't need words to communicate. At least, that is how he felt. Once breakfast was over, he rinsed the plates and she set them in the dishwasher. He yawned.

She laughed. "Sleepy? You could crash here if you want."

"Yeah, I was thinking about it." He could smell the fragrance that enveloped her. Her hair hung down, just past her shoulders. He rarely ever saw her hair loose like this, as Janay preferred the practicality of wearing her hair in a ponytail. Her liquid, black eyes were full of compassion. His hands moved as if of their own accord and he placed them around her waist.

"Thank you. I can't tell you how much it meant that you were there for me."

"It's all right."

He couldn't take his gaze off her. Her face, scrubbed clean, glowed. Her lips beckoned him. "No, it's not. Not everyone would have done it. You'll never know who you are to me."

"You know me." She grinned. "I'll collect sooner or later."

He wasn't sure which one of them made the first move. But they were in each other's arms. The brief contact set him on fire. It felt like an electric current pulsing through his veins. He knew he wasn't in this alone. He knew she could feel it too—the same surge of electricity. That explained why she'd shuddered—although almost unnoticeably—a split-second ago.

What if she was just as hungry for him as he was for her? The possibility brought with it a maddening sensation that had his head spinning with a rush of adrenaline. It was overwhelming yet calming. It spurred him to take her; to make her his without any sliver of hesitation.

She stared deep into his eyes, her eyes almost pleading. Her eyes were soft, mirroring his. Locking eyes with her, he lowered his head toward hers. Her lips slowly parted, unsettling the fine hairs on his upper lip with a streak of hot breath. And his lips—they seemed to have a mind of their own, because they reached for hers and wrapped around them.

He closed his eyes, shutting out every image so he could focus on the pleasure she brought him. He dragged his lips along her lower lip; it was a lot softer than he'd thought. A lot softer than it looked.

Her lips moved slowly, following his lead.

Thoughts came creeping into his head, but he banished them at once. Yes, he had kissed her without a second thought, but he didn't want to think about what he was doing. There would be no point in finding the logic of it. This was illogical and spontaneous. Maybe he would never get another chance to taste her lips again, so all he wanted was to live the moment.

The kiss was slow and soft. He wouldn't be surprised if she pulled away, but she didn't. She grasped his arm and deepened the kiss, her lips becoming firmer around his. Her breath grew heavier, disclosing her need for more of him. Her breath merged with his, making the air around them heavy with desire.

He snaked his tongue out of his mouth and ran it along her lower lip as though seeking permission to enter her. She welcomed him with a sultry smile, parting her lips even further to let him in. He pushed through her lips, his tongue meeting hers in an erotic dance. He could hear her desperation in her now raspy voice as she moaned against his lips. He could feel it in her eager fingers as they explored his arm.

He could feel his muscles bulging beneath her palm. His muscles weren't the only things bulging though. There was another, sandwiched between their heated bodies. Enlarging with each breath he sucked in, he soon felt it straining against his pants.

She gasped, her lips pulling away from his. She had felt it when he poked her with his erection.

"Fitz," she whispered.

Fitz's eyes narrowed, and then they settled on her amorous eyes. He stared at her, waiting for a reaction, but there was none. Yes, she loved being with him. But did she want *this*?

He'd be lying if he said he knew. He stared deep into her eyes in a bid to see through her, but although her eyes were soft and enchanting, they didn't give anything away. Need burned like fire in his muscles and nerves. After denying this for so long, he couldn't contain himself. So, he hoped she wouldn't stop him.

When her body remained glued to his, hope flared in his heart. He snaked his arms around her and leaned forward as though he would kiss her again. She straightened her spine, her eyes fixed on his lips as they advanced toward hers, but he went for her left ear instead, teasing it with his breath.

He caught her earlobe between his lips and gently tugged at it. "I want you, Janay."

His voice was barely a breath, but he knew she'd heard him. He buried his face in the crook of her neck and started to overwhelm her with feathery kisses.

She moaned, holding on to him as though her legs would give way if she dared let go. "Oh, Fitz. Ye..."

She trailed off, her voice lost in pleasure. That was a yes, Fitz knew that. But he needed to hear her say it.

"Hmm?" He kissed his way back to her earlobe, covering her skin inch by inch. "Is that a yes?"

His left hand found the globes of her ass. He squeezed hard.

"Yes, Fitz!" She moaned as he squeezed harder. "Please..."

There. That was the go-ahead he needed.

He gingerly lifted her into his arms and headed for the living room. The bedroom was too far for what he had in mind, so he lay her on the steel-gray rug in the living room. She lay motionless, her eyes devouring him as she awaited his next move.

He went straight for her clothes and started to peel them off her skin.

Once she was fully unclad, he paused for a moment to take in every detail of her sensuality. Her body was far more perfect than he had imagined. Her long, sensuous curves and smooth, dark brown skin simply took his breath away.

There was something about the way her eyes gleamed from beneath long lashes. It drove him wild with need, spurring him to rid himself of his clothes. Her eyes burned into him as he undressed, fueling the raging fire deep inside of him. He tossed off his clothes and went for the prize, his large body pinning her to the floor.

Her hips bucked as she adjusted to his weight, and almost immediately, her legs wrapped around him, pulling him close. He brushed a strand of hair away from her face just before his lips captured hers again.

How could I have denied myself this woman for so long?

His fingers crawled down the sides of her body, and when he reached the soft curves of her curvy hips, they settled there, gently teasing. His lips were hot against hers, the fiery kiss invoking a blistering lust that was hard to contain. He trailed a line of kisses down her throat and onto her shoulder. Her scent, a delicious concoction of vanilla and coconut, raised his libido up a notch. The nipples on her breasts stood up rosy and proud. He took a swollen bud in his mouth, savoring the taste and shape of it. She gasped loudly. He suckled on one. Tingles of desire wound their way down to his belly and his erection thickened in response.

Her fingers speared through his hair, keeping his mouth pinned to her breast as if she couldn't bear it if he stopped. He sensed her need as surely as he did his.

With his knee, he nudged her legs apart. His tip hovered on the sweet spot that was already wet and moist. She arched her back under the tender assault. With a quick thrust of his hips, he shoved his way in. She gasped, her grip on his hair instinctively tightening as her muscles clenched around him.

A few deep breaths was all she needed to relax her tensed muscles. They slowly expanded, stretching to accommodate his length and girth. She moaned with pleasure as he started to thrust, slow and deep. Her breath was hot against his mouth, her lips greedy for more of his kisses. So he claimed her lips again. They were fused together, lip to lip, toe to toe, as intimately as possible. Their bodies rocked together, dancing to their heartbeats.

He picked up pace. She didn't object. Rapidly, almost desperately, he stroked in and out. Now bordering on speed, he only made it mid-way inside of her before thrusting out. Her natural lube glistened around his hardness, joining his own fluid to form a perfect blend.

Janay matched him. No other woman completed him like she did. No other woman had ever driven him to such dizzying heights of passion. But here he was, drunk on her. The yearning for release started to build up inside him, taking him higher and higher on the wild ride. He pounded harder, his hardness thickening as he swayed on the brink of the steep abyss. Still, he waited as she gasped and moaned. He pushed her higher, faster, harder until finally she cried out as the orgasm hit her like a tornado. Her cry was soft, yet it dripped with the purest blend of pleasure. The contractions of her inner walls sought to slow him down, but he kept going, savoring the feel of her breasts massaging his chest.

Only when he felt the contractions lessen did he extricate himself from inside her. He was on the edge of his orgasm, so he wrapped his fingers around his shaft and started to stroke himself. She lay there on her back, watching him with intrigue. He moaned as the first wave of orgasm hit him.

Then Janay did something amazing, she arched her slender back, offering herself as a living gift to him. Her whole body seemed to say 'take me'. The expression in her eyes gave him an unspoken permission. Permission to spill his essence on her.

He filled her with his girth once again, slipping through the wetness until he could go no further. And then he flooded her with his seed. He groaned from the sheer pleasure of it and then he collapsed from utter exertion, despite his almost maniacal fitness regimen.

For a long while, they stayed together, silent.

What did he just do? Whatever he did was the most amazing experience of his life.

Yet, it might have ruined the one thing he treasured above all—her friendship. He'd also spoiled his entire plan and risked her love. She was coming around, he'd felt sure of it. Now, what would happen after what they experienced together? What did she feel about it?

He wanted to ask her so many questions but no words escaped his lips. It felt terrible to not be able to talk to the woman with whom he used to discuss everything under the sun.

Would he lose her forever? He sure hoped not. He prayed this was not so.

Now, that he tasted her, he could never leave her alone. He loved her, totally and irrevocably. She was his sun, his moon, his everything. Then, if she didn't understand it, perhaps the best thing to do would be to move somewhere far, far away, so he could live alone with the pain in his heart.

If he couldn't have her, he didn't want anything or anyone else.

CHRISTMAS CUPID

Chapter Seven

While they both lay there, shock and pain coursed through Janay's veins. She felt utterly ashamed of her own behavior. Fitz was at his most vulnerable now, given the fact that he'd barely escaped losing his mother. Naturally, he wasn't thinking straight. She should've maintained control of the situation. How could she make love to him so wantonly? He was her best friend. Did she ruin the relationship they shared for such a long time?

Losing him would kill her.

She didn't want that—ever.

So, how could they continue to be friends after making love? They'd crossed the line; friends don't have sex with friends. It's an absolute no-no. She would never consider having *Fitz with benefits,* even though they'd just had sex that still boggled her mind. Yes, she felt more than confused. On the one hand, she wanted to beg him to consider her as his girlfriend. For too long, she fought the attraction—but no longer could she deny her feelings for Fitz. They ran true and deep. On the other hand, he'd been thinking along the lines of settling down and he'd possibly found the person to do that with. Maria. He seemed to be genuinely interested in her. How could she come between them when she'd been the one who set them up?

And yet, this is exactly what she just did.

Shame and regret roiled inside her in equal measure. She hated to feel this way. Why, oh why, didn't she put a stop to this before it got to this point? So massively stupid of her to put him in such a difficult position. She sat up, gathered her clothes and hurried into her bedroom. When she came back, showered and dressed, he was sitting at the kitchen table.

"I've got to get to work."

His expression looked incredulous. "You don't have any gigs today. Remember?"

Damn it!

She forgot about that, but no way would she sit here talking about what just happened. He would tell her it'd been a mistake and that would just kill her. She couldn't face his rejection. Not when she harbored such strong feelings for him. How could she have been silly enough to assume she would be happy being just his friend?

She loved him.

She couldn't admit it to him, though. He would brush her feelings aside. This was probably nothing more than sex for him, but for her, it'd been the culmination of all her emotions. It would be better to get out before she lost whatever little sense she still possessed and blurted out her love for him. She needed to get away before she made this worse. "I just remembered that I've some urgent work in the office."

"We should sit and talk…"

She didn't quite look at him as she picked up her purse and keys. "Some other time, Fitz. I really have to go. Would you please let yourself out and close the door? It will lock automatically."

He stood, looking flabbergasted. "But…"

She rushed out before he could stop her. Swiftly, she took the stairs and strode down. Of course, she didn't have to report to work today. The office was closed. She could go out and sit in a café until she was sure he'd left her place. Damn it, why go to such hassles when she had better options? She stopped at the second floor and pressed the bell.

Lexi opened the door. "Hi. Come in. Brielle and I were discussing the wedding plans while we decorated the Christmas tree."

Janay rushed in and closed the door. "Is Cole around?"

Lexi cocked an eyebrow. She moved to take the tinsel from Brielle's hands. "No. He went to the grocery store. Why? What's wrong?" Her eyes widened. "Fitz's mother?"

Janay dropped on the couch. "No, she's doing well. It's—I need to talk about something personal."

Brielle hung a carnation-red ball on the tree. She stepped back to admire it. "What is it?"

Janay dropped her head in her hands. "I just made the biggest mistake of my life."

After draping the tinsel on the tree, Lexi came over to rub her back. "What is it, sweetie? It can't be that bad."

"Oh! It's worse than what you think. Much worse!" She gulped and pressed her hands to her eyes. Tears threatened to slide down but she choked them back. What if she lost Fitz forever? Without him, she would be lost. He wasn't just a friend, he was much more. Now, when she really considered the possibility that she might never see him again, it hit her full on—he was the anchor in her life. She depended on him. More than that, she loved him. Not as a friend, but as a man with whom she could easily imagine spending her life with. "I've ruined everything."

"What have you done? Murder?" Lexi joked.

"Worse than that!" she admitted.

"Tell us everything. Don't keep it inside you." Leaving the tree and the decorations that lay waiting in the box, Brielle gripped her hands. "Whatever it is, we'll be there for you."

"I—I slept with Fitz."

Her sisters simply stared at her.

She could understand their shock. They literally saw Fitz grow up with her. In their eyes, he was like a brother they never had. How could she have done something like this? How could she make them understand what she felt for him was far more than just brotherly? If she told them, she loved him, would they understand? She doubted it. No one would be able to comprehend how she could have felt like this and never realized the depths of her own emotions.

"You—slept with Randy?" Brielle asked in a quiet voice.

Janay nodded and couldn't quite meet their eyes.

Lexi snickered. Catching Brielle's fulminating gaze, she stopped. "Sorry."

"Tell us how it happened," Brielle ordered.

From the beginning, she told the whole tale of how she set him up with other women. Then about how they began to spend time together, so she could get to know him more. She told them about going to the fair and the various others times they went out. Then she explained about the women she chose for him. "He likes this new girl, Maria. She's actually perfect for him. Beautiful, too."

Lexi opened her mouth, then closed it. "Umm? What did Randy say after you guys did it?"

Janay winced. She could recall with perfect alacrity his horrified expression when she rushed out. He would never see her again, she felt sure of it. "I didn't give him a chance to talk. Afterwards, I just left."

"So, he still might be upstairs?" Lexi glanced up as if she could sense him.

"I don't know. He probably left."

"But to me this sounds like—" Lexi stopped when Brielle gave her a menacing look. "I see. Hmm...this is strange."

"Strange isn't how I would describe it. Mad. Crazy. Stupid!" Janay banged her hands on the counter. "How could I have been so reckless?"

Much to her surprise, Brielle began to laugh.

Janay glared at her sister. Was she actually making fun of her?

How could she?

Brielle always acted like the compassionate and considerate one in the family.

Janay expected more support from her.

Brielle wiped her eyes. "Sorry. It just reminds me of that stupid thing I did to Toby."

"This is totally different."

"So? You love him, don't you?" Lexi asked her.

Lexi's question took her breath away. Of course, she should've known her sisters would be able to see through her in an instant. "Yes, but there's a difference. Toby also loved Brielle. Fitz thinks of me as a friend."

"But when he asked you to set him up..." Lexi started again.

Brielle shook her head with warning.

Lexi halted. "I—well, I think you should have a serious talk with him."

"I wouldn't know where to begin."

"Maybe you should let him make the next move."

"He'll probably never want to see me again," she whined.

"I wouldn't worry about that." Lexi waved a hand. "I mean, you've been friends for a long time. He wouldn't want to put an end to your relationship so quickly."

"I don't know..." Janay stood. "...I'm just tired. Maybe, I need some sleep and then I can think about this."

"You'll have to deal with it at some point," Brielle urged. "If he's still upstairs—?"

"I can't." Tears slid down her cheeks. "Lexi, can I crash in your guest room?"

"Sure, sweetie." Lexi hugged her.

Janay dragged her feet to the bedroom and crawled into bed. Even though her mind was running active, her body felt more tired than she realized. Within minutes, she fell fast asleep. She woke up two hours later and a casual search around Lexi's apartment, revealed what she'd already suspected, judging by the relative silence of the place. No one was in the house, except her. The Christmas tree was ablaze with fairy lights. A white, snowy angel peered at her from the top of it. She found Lexi's note on the counter. She and Brielle had gone out to buy some stuff for the wedding. Janay felt a pang of guilt. She'd been so wrapped up in her own problems that she forgot the various twists and turns of her sisters' lives. Once she dealt with Fitz, she would start paying more attention to them. She trudged to her apartment, but not before making sure she'd locked Lexi's door.

She tried to open her door, but it was locked. This meant that Fitz had eventually left. *Thank god.* She wasn't ready to face him, not yet. She dug into her handbag for her keys and unlocked the door. She was right, Fitz wasn't here. She inhaled a deep breath and then exhaled it sharply.

Rather than waste time, she dragged out her Christmas decorations. She sorted through them to see if she had enough. Of course, she would have to get a tree. Maybe she could enlist Toby or Cole to help her pick out one. *Tomorrow.* She didn't have the energy to do it today. After dawdling about in the house for hours, she felt bored. Maybe she would go and catch a movie.

The whole weekend turned into a total loss. Although, she did manage to get a tree on Sunday, she wasn't able to concentrate on anything other than her own confused emotions. Fitz called a few times but she let the calls go to voicemail. He left messages. She didn't respond. At some point, she would have to deal with the situation but for now, she needed a break.

Janay threw herself into her work with renowned vigor. A few days later, she went to the hospital to check on the progress of Fitz's mother. Since visiting hours were open, she was allowed to see her for ten minutes.

Elena pressed her hand.

She should've come earlier, but she didn't want to risk running into Fitz. "Sorry, I couldn't come before…"

"You're too sweet, dear. But don't worry about me. I'm going to be home before Christmas."

Janay doubted that she would be allowed to go home so quickly, but she tried to give Elena an encouraging smile. Once she left the room, she headed out. Much to her consternation, she ran into Fitz.

He was carrying a bouquet of white roses. He stopped in mid-stride when he spotted her. "Hi."

She shifted the strap of her purse, still not quite feeling up to meeting his eyes. How she missed him! His absence became an ache in her heart that wouldn't go away. By god, why didn't she ever realize before that he meant so much to her? She longed to throw herself into his arms and confess her love, but of course, she couldn't do that. "Umm—hi, Fitz. Your mom is doing better."

"How are you?"

"I'm fine." What the hell was this? Were they doomed to make small talk now? This is just crazy. Maybe it was stupid of her to avoid him. She should've just pretended she wasn't affected by their lovemaking but it was too late to do that now. "Umm—how's Maria?" *Shit!* Janay resisted the urge to slap her hand on her forehead. How could she have asked about the girl he was currently dating, just days after making love to him?

"She's fine." He smiled. "We're meeting tomorrow for a date."

Jealousy immediately reared its ugly head. Along with another emotion—anger. He acted so casual. How could he make love to her and then turn around and date another woman? Didn't he have some morals and values? The shock of his statement made her straighten her spine. The man was a jerk! She'd been wrong to solely blame herself for this mishap. He was just as responsible for this mess. "Really? Where?" She knew her voice sounded sugary sweet, but inside rage bubbled like molten lava—and when it spewed, God help him, because no one else would be able to do anything to save him from her ire.

"At Devon's. About six." He smiled, looking idiotically happy. "She's great. Thanks, Janay. You really chose well when you introduced us."

Janay wanted to throttle him. "Yeah." She nodded. All she wanted to do was leave before she hit him on the head with something. How could he be with another woman when he'd leapt into her arms without as much as a murmur of protest? "I've got to go."

Fritz made no attempt to stop her or talk about their not-so-innocent activities over the weekend. "See you around." Whistling happily, he left.

Janay snarled after he departed. She wanted to punch him, yell and scream but what good would it do? *No! The man needs a punishment worthy of his crime.* She would think of something suitable.

Fritz wouldn't know what hit him.

Now, Janay was on a mission.

CHRISTMAS CUPID

Chapter Eight

His arrow must have hit the bull's-eye. Fitz felt sure an explosion was about to happen. Janay wasn't the sort to take things lying down for long. She would be along soon enough, ready to teach him a lesson.

Until then, he could sit tight and perfect his plan.

His mind wandered to other thoughts. Feeling a bit relieved at his mother's recovery, Fitz ordered a drink as he waited for his date to arrive. Soon, she'd be out of the hospital and he could go back to his normal life. Of course, he intended to spend a little more time with her now, since she suffered from such a close call. His mother was a strong, independent woman who hated to rely on others, but he would have to force her to accept some help.

As always, Janay gave him a good idea when she told him to hire a full-time housekeeper for his mom. The investments his father left in his mother's name ensured there would be enough income for her to afford the help. And if she made a fuss, he would just have to pay for it himself. Whatever the case, he didn't want to worry about her being alone in the house.

"Scary thoughts?" Maria asked as she joined him. "You look tense."

He smiled. "Just worrying about my mother."

"How's she doing?"

"Better." He nodded to another friend who passed. This was one of his favorite haunts and he knew many of the regulars. "So, what would you like to order?"

"A martini, please."

Fitz walked over to get her drink. When he came back, she was in deep conversation on the phone. He waited until she finished. "Thank you for coming tonight. I know it's a lot to ask."

"It's for a good cause." She laughed. "But are you sure—"

"There's Janay." Fitz waved. "Hey!"

"Hi." Janay joined them. Dressed in a raspberry-red, curve-hugging dress, she looked fabulous. Gold earrings dangled from her ears. Her dark hair spilled down, a little passed her shoulders, and her eyes glowed with ill-concealed anger. "I forgot you guys were coming here."

"What are you doing here?" Fitz feigned surprise.

Of course, he expected her to turn up to take a look at him and Maria. Did he imagine for a minute, she would take things lightly when he slept with her and then dated another woman?

No way! Not his Janay. He felt amazed she didn't scratch his eyes out. She wasn't the most patient or docile person on the planet...just the way he liked her.

Liked? No, he loved her. Loved her spunk, her sheer guts and nerve...her compassion. But she wasn't feeling compassionate right now. He could bet on that. Her eyes threw invisible darts. She was near to bursting with fury—and he intended to push her over the edge.

She raised an eyebrow and gave him a haughty stare. "You know I come here fairly often."

"On weeknights?" he questioned.

"Sure, why not? You know me. I'm the soul of a party." She shrugged and turned her attention to Maria. "How are you doing?"

"Great...great."

Janay opened her mouth to say something, but Fitz put his hand on Maria's. "That's my favorite song. Would you like to dance?"

"Sure." Maria glided away with him to the dance floor.

While he swayed with her, Fitz kept a stealthy gaze trained at Janay who was throwing them dirty looks. It looked pretty obvious that she was jealous. Why else would she turn up here? It wouldn't be wise to let her know he was on to her. She wouldn't take it kindly. But then his woman brought this mess right down on her own lap, because she couldn't accept that she loved him

How difficult was it to admit it?

He would take a particular delight in letting her know he loved her as much as she did him. But he would have to bide his time. This wasn't the right moment. She needed to be ripe to hear what he wanted to say. He danced with Maria, taking pleasure in the way Janay's eyes grew smoking hot seeing him with the other woman. When he led her back to the table, Janay sat sipping her beer. Despite the nonchalant expression on her face, he could tell she was really pissed off. He knew her well enough to gauge her mood and she looked quite near to blowing off steam. "Hey, Janay, guess what? Maria just got promoted."

"Wow! Congratulations!" Janay replied. Her glance settled on his date. "This calls for a celebration."

"Yeah, it sure does." Fitz grabbed Maria's hand and planted a kiss on it. "What would be an appropriate promotion gift?"

"You don't have to give me a gift."

"I think you've earned it."

Maria's gaze wandered to the bar. "Hey! I know that girl. We used to work together. Let me go say hi."

When she sauntered off, he picked up his drink. "So, what's new with you?"

Janay nibbled on her bottom lip.

God! She looked gorgeous when she was in a flaming mood. He longed to take her in his arms and kiss her senseless. The memory of their time together flashed through his mind.

Once wasn't enough.

He wanted more.

"Nothing's on my mind," she snapped.

"Thanks for visiting my mom. She was very happy to see you."

"I like her."

"And the feeling is mutual," he assured her, although he could tell she only made conversation to kill time. Normally, she was the heart and soul of a group. Tonight however, she was off her game. Of course, she only came here to check out the chemistry between him and Maria. Now, since she'd done just that, he expected her to make an excuse and disappear. Knowing her, she would simmer inside for a week or so, and then explode into a terrible tantrum. That's when he would tell her he loved her with a fervor he couldn't describe.

Another week! Wait for one more week. He reminded himself. It was important to be patient, at least for that long.

"Lexi's having a tough time. Another client cancelled today," she said. "We're all upset but she took it really hard since she's the one who actually deals with the clients."

"You're sure it's Arianna."

"Positive," she confirmed. "Cole poked around a bit. One of her acquaintances said Arianna's determined to destroy Lexi's life because she thinks Lexi stole her man."

Fitz felt incensed. "She left him at the dammed altar."

"The woman is mentally unstable."

It enraged him to think that someone could destroy the sisters' hard work with such little effort. It was unfair. "If you could link her to the rumors, I could give you the name of a good lawyer who would sue her ass for defamation. She can't get away with it."

"That's what I'm thinking about. Lexi and Cole are in such a happy place. I hate that someone is managing to ruin their joy and peace of mind. If I saw that woman..." Her fingers tightened on the bottle. "But she's already been to a court and the message didn't sink in."

"So, what are you planning?" Knowing her, there was a plan bubbling inside. Arianna didn't know what was in store for her.

The woman is doomed.

His Janay was a deadly weapon—and he couldn't wait to see her in action.

"I want to confront her," she admitted. "She wouldn't like that. Liars never do. And it would serve the best results if I could do it in a place where there are a lot of people she knows. She wouldn't even expect us to corner her in a public place. When she becomes aware that we are on to her, she would have to let go of her silly plans."

"It's a good idea. If I can be of help, let me know."

"I'm still mulling over things. First, I need to talk it over with Lexi and Brielle to see what they say. But it might be difficult to corner her in a public place. We don't exactly move in the same social circles."

"Then make her circle yours."

She snorted. "How do we do that?"

"If you're managing an event where she's invited, you'll most likely run into her."

Janay's mouth gaped open. She gazed at him as if seeing him for the first time. "That's actually a brilliant plan. And I have the perfect event in mind." Her eyes danced with glee. "The Rogers would go for that. They were pretty angry after she made fools of them and fed them lies about us. It might actually work."

He nodded. "Yeah, it could. And if you need my help, don't hesitate to call."

They went silent as they both got busy with their own thoughts. Once, they could have talked for hours, but now awkwardness prevailed between them. He hated this newfound unease. With Janay, he always felt comfortable. But now, it wasn't the same. Soon, he promised himself. He would tell her everything and things would be better than before.

She finished her beer. "I should go," she said.

He leaned over. "I'm planning to go home to Maria's apartment," he added as a parting shot.

"Good for you!" She snarled. "Hope she doesn't wear you out. Bye." She turned to leave, but Maria stood just a few feet away.

"Leaving so soon?"

"Yeah. I—just need to go." She strode off.

Fitz couldn't contain his grin. *Perfect!* He expected to see her in a few more days. She wouldn't wait too long.

"So, when is this mystery girl coming?" Maria asked as she took a seat.

Fitz cleared his throat. He hadn't told her that Janay was the girl. All he told her was how he loved another girl and wanted to make her a bit jealous by allowing her to see him with Maria. He made a show of flipping his wrist to check the time and frowned. "Looks like she might be a little late. Maybe she isn't coming, after all. I guess we should head out too."

Maria plucked out her phone from her silver clutch. "Okay. Good. I'll call Adam. We have a date for tomorrow." She looked unsure, then returned her phone back into her clutch. "It's too noisy here. I'll call when we're outside."

He admired the ease with which she fell into a relationship with another guy after their first disastrous date. He didn't see her again until today. All his fibs to Janay were harmless. He never dated Maria, but she'd agreed to help him out tonight. They strode outside.

Maria dialed a number. By the time they stepped out, she was already making plans. "Yeah, baby! I'll see you tomorrow. Seven is perfect. It's a date." She laughed.

Janay stood right outside.

Fitz's heart slammed into his chest.

Busted!

Hearing Maria's conversation, she raised an eyebrow. "You have a date?"

Fitz tried to warn Maria but her back was turned towards him. *Shit!* He didn't expect Janay to catch on so quickly. "Hey!" he said in an effort to distract the women.

"Hey," Maria answered Janay.

They were too involved to take notice of him.

"Yeah. It was my new guy," Maria admitted as she shoved the phone back in her purse.

"Boyfriend?" Janay spluttered. "But aren't you dating Fitz?"

"Didn't Fitz tell you? We like each other...but not like that. Sorry! I guess he just didn't want to break your heart by letting you know that this particular matchmaking effort didn't bring any results."

"What do you mean?"

"I suppose this isn't a failure on your efforts, but rather Fitz's fault. He should have told you that he likes someone else."

Fitz felt the urge to slap his forehead. Women! Why did they have to talk with each other? How the hell was he supposed to get out of this mess now? "Maria is just talking nonsense." He stood and put his hand on Maria's shoulder as a warning.

Finally understanding she was doing something wrong, Maria stiffened. "Sorry! I didn't realize that she—Oh! Never mind. I think I should leave."

Fitz watched his fake date slip away. She caught a cab and zoomed off. Now, he was really in for it.

It'd been stupid of him to push her so fast and so hard. He should've been more careful. It might have been a good idea to at least warn Maria that Janay didn't know about what he was doing, about how Janay *was* the woman he wanted to make jealous. Well, it was too late for regrets now. The way Janay was glaring at him he was really in for a world of pain.

She wouldn't let him go very easily.

Now, he would have to think fast on his feet.

Chapter Nine

Her heart pulsated with a deep, thriving need to slap him, but she controlled the temptation. Fitz was playing some kind of a convoluted game she couldn't even understand, let alone unravel.

She intended to get to the bottom of this mystery—fast! *What the hell is he doing?*

With her hand on her hips, she glowered.

He had the audacity to look casual, like nothing was wrong. "What?"

"We need to talk." Her voice sounded harsh even to her own ears. As always, she took control of the situation. Shying away from a confrontation wasn't her style. After she made love to him, she should've dealt with the situation. But it'd been the shock that made her lose her nerve. She'd already allowed things to fester for too long.

Now, she would be taking charge.

And boy, oh boy! He's in for a rough night.

He followed her out into a tiny alcove next to the main entrance of the bar. The wind that hit her might have been cold, but Janay didn't bother to button her coat. The anger simmering deep inside her was fiery enough to keep her warm. "Who the hell is this woman that you're in love with?"

Fitz took a deep breath. His dancing eyes sparkled in the dim light of the bulb that hung over the door.

Both of them didn't break the eye contact.

"All right. I didn't tell you—I'm in love with someone else."

"That much I gathered, you moron! Who is she?"

"Uh—you don't know her that well."

"But I know her?" she snarled.

"Sort of, yes."

She didn't know what the hell he was talking about. How could she know someone 'sort of'? "What's her name?"

"Look..." He shoved his hands inside the pockets of his jacket. "...I don't want to talk about it. Since I haven't told her yet, I think it's kind of meaningless to tell others."

"You told Maria!"

"That's different." Fitz shrugged. "I needed her help to make this woman jealous."

"So, you used her?"

"With her consent," he countered. "You shouldn't get so worked up about it. Maria knew right from the start. I should've told her not to mention anything to you."

She opened her mouth to say something snarky, but then snapped it shut. No words came out, even though she wanted to tell him a million things. After he slept with her, he had the nerve to admit he was actually in love with someone else? Was he crazy? How could she not react to that? But she couldn't say all that. Janay didn't want him to know how badly she was affected by his cold and callous behavior. Sure, their lovemaking happened as an on-the-spur-of-the-moment kind of a thing. He was vulnerable at that time. She was stupid. But still, there was a certain code of conduct that needed to be maintained and yet, he made no attempt to do so.

"You told me to fix you up with Maria and with all these other women. If you knew that you were in love with another person, why didn't you just ask me to help you get her attention?"

He rubbed his forehead, glanced away and then back at her. "Janay, I just don't want to talk about it."

"You don't want to talk about it?" Her voice rose up quite a few octaves. Janay could feel the build-up of furious energy spiraling sharply inside her. How dare he dismiss her! "You don't want to talk about it?" she repeated.

His eyes narrowed at her shrill voice. "Don't take that tone with me."

He sounded like a school headmaster chiding her for being rude. But she was now past the point of rational thinking. She tried long enough, but it wasn't working. How could she maintain her cool when the opposite party—Mister Randy Fitzgerald—seemed bent on being the world's biggest dim-wit? Insensitive Jerk! "And don't you dare set me aside after sleeping with me!"

Damn it! She didn't want to drag this particular issue into their fight. Sure, it was the real reason why she felt bothered by this whole mess, but she didn't want him to know that.

She was mad at him and he needed to know that much.

He scowled. "So, that's what it's all about?"

"Sure it is," she spat out the words as if they were poison. "And why shouldn't it be? You made love to me and then—and then—you have the gall to declare that you have always been in love with this...weird, invisible woman?"

"She's not weird." He pointed a finger at her. "Don't call her names."

"And don't you dare refuse to talk to me when you damn well know that you owe me an explanation," she snarled. Janay was well aware that she was acting emotionally. And why shouldn't she? She was in love with this thoughtless, tactless jerk who didn't have the decency to come right out and admit his true feelings for another woman before he made love to her. Why couldn't he have put a stop to it when she made the move? Or did he make the first move? She wasn't sure.

But somehow or the other, it's all his fault.

Of course, it is!

So, she wasn't going to let him off the hook that easily.

"I wanted us to talk, remember. You're the one who walked out," he fired back. His nostrils flared and a muscle ticked in his cheek.

She never saw him this angry before. *Good!* She wanted to rile him up, just like he managed to do to her.

"We should've discussed this right then and there. But no! You wanted to pretend that nothing happened."

"Nothing *significant* happened," she shot back.

He took a threatening step forward. "Then why are you making such a big fuss about it now?"

As he loomed large over her, she realized for the first time that he was quite a bit taller than her. Bulkier, too. But this was Fitz, the gentlest soul on earth. She'd always been the one who exploded like a volcano on occasion. He always acted cool and composed. Right now though, in his current state of mind, he seemed a little bit scary. A bit dangerous, too.

In a sexy sort of way!

No, *no* she wasn't going to think along those lines.

Get a grip, Janay.

"I didn't know that you were in love with another woman before—I allowed you to lay your hands on me."

"Why does that make a difference?"

Janay spluttered with shock. *Is he a complete moron? How could that not matter?* He put his hands on her, touched her in the most intimate manner and all the while, he was secretly in love with another woman? The insult burned in her heart like a flame. "It makes a big difference. If you're in love with someone, you should be faithful to them."

Hearing her words, he shook his head. Befuddlement shone in his eyes. "We're veering way off topic. Let's just take some time to cool down. We can talk about this later."

He made sense. Their friendship was too old and strong to be adversely affected by these tiring circumstances. In a normal situation, Janay would have agreed to talk about this at a later day. But a storm raged in her mind that refused to die down.

He made love to her.

She loved him.

Sure, it was her problem and she would deal with it. But he also needed to shoulder some responsibility. Why couldn't he accept his mistake? If he only told her who the girl was, she might be able to make some peace with this ridiculous situation. But no...he seemed determined to protect her identity. "Just tell me her name," she ordered. This matter needed to be resolved, at least a little bit in her head before she could make sense of the rest of it.

"I can't. Please try to understand. She's the one who needs to hear those words from me first...not someone else."

Tears burned her eyes, but she refused to let them spill. The insult hit her straight in the heart and throbbed like a barb that was stuck there. "So, I'm *someone else* now?"

He grabbed her hand and pressed it to his heart. "No! You're not."

She jerked it free. Her emotions were all over the place. Even though she felt deeply hurt over the fact of how he could just dismiss her with such ease after sleeping with her, she might have been able to take that wound, if he didn't rub salt on it by brushing aside their years of friendship. Nothing mattered to him.

She didn't matter and neither did their old bond. The truth hurt like a bitch! Still, she needed to hear it from him. "Now, that you've found this amazing wonder woman, there's no place in your life for an old friend? Is that it?"

"Oh, babe. Don't say that." He raised a hand to touch her cheek. "You're important to me."

She snorted. Those damned tears continued to prickle at the back of her eyes, but she pushed them back. She would never give him the satisfaction of seeing her cry. How could she have thought he was her best friend? How could she have slept with him? Friends don't sleep with friends and worse than all that, she loved him from the depths of her heart and yet, he acted callous and insulting. She'd been a fool to fall in love with a man whose eyes were trained on another woman. It was all her fault. She should've taken more care with her heart. Her heart felt like it was breaking into a million pieces and there wasn't a damn thing she could do about it.

"Goodbye!" The word sounded so final that she actually felt something break inside her when she uttered it. She turned away. There wasn't anything else left for her to say.

He rushed after her. "Janay! Wait!"

She didn't want to hear anymore. What else could he say? There wasn't anything that could wipe the anguish stabbing through every fiber and vein in her body. She felt the pain almost as if it was a physical ailment. She hailed a cab and collapsed into it. Even though, Fitz tried to open the door, she told the driver to drive off.

If he wanted to say something else, she didn't want to hear it. All she wanted to do was go home and cry her eyes out. Perhaps once she got this pain out of her system, she would be able to resume her friendship.

Or perhaps—it was dead forever.

She didn't know. All she knew was that the only man she ever loved was in love with another woman—and there wasn't a damn thing she could do about it.

This was the end of things, the end of an era. She didn't intend to see Fitz ever again.

It's over.

For two whole days, Janay felt more miserable than ever before. Despite her best efforts, she couldn't get him out of her mind. He would sneak in too, the conniving fellow he was—into her thoughts and heart whenever she let down her guard. She wanted to get over him. She wanted to move on. How could she though, when he called all day, sent her text messages, banged against her door, even enlisted the help of her sisters to get her to talk to him? She ignored them all. Maybe she should start seeing someone else. Maybe she needed to get out of the city.

Do something! Someone shrieked in her head. She'd been unable to galvanize herself into any action though. She hated inaction more than anything. She couldn't just allow herself to wallow in grief when she wasn't the one who did anything wrong. Fitz was out there, probably on a date with this woman, maybe seeing her every day, basking in the glory of his newfound love and she kept moaning over the idiot.

She couldn't allow him to get away with hurting her in such a callous manner.

She wouldn't allow him to do it.

It wasn't just the insult that pissed her off, but rather the unknown, unfamiliar feelings swirling in her heart. How could she not have realized that she loved him all this time? Whenever the thought rose in her head, she pushed it away. Now it was too late.

Why did she accept her own emotions, only after she lost him?

What could she do about this miserable situation?

Misery didn't suit her. She needed to do something. Without some action, she would go mad. On Christmas Eve, she banged on Fitz's door. She'd had enough. One way or the other, she was going to settle things. She loved Fitz. Madly. Completely. She'd become determined to fight for him.

One thing now became crystal clear in her head; whoever the woman was, she wasn't worthy of his love. No one could love Fitz like she loved him. Didn't the man see it? How could he miss what stared him in the face? Once he realized she loved him, it would only be a matter of time for him to come to the same conclusion.

Well, he just needed a push—she was here to deliver it.

When he opened the door, Fitz blinked as if he was seeing her for the first time in forever. "Janay, what a surprise!"

"Yeah, isn't it?" she said dryly. Without an invitation, she strode in. Was the conniving woman here? Had he told her about them? Was she reveling in the glory of his love? Well, she was here to crush the woman's dreams. Fitz was hers—hers alone. No one would snatch him away. The living room was empty except for the cheery Christmas tree that glowed in one corner, a pile of presents already stacked under it. His sock hung alone on the fireplace. *Good!* At least, things weren't serious enough for the woman to earn her own sock in his house. "Are you alone?"

"Yes, I am. If you're here to ask me about that woman again—"

"I'm not." She poked her index finger against his chest. "I don't give a fuck who she is. All I know is she's wrong for you."

His eyebrows rose and his lips pressed together. "And how do you know that without even knowing who she is?"

"Because..." Janay faltered. She needed to compose herself. She gulped deeply. After coming this far, she wasn't backing off. It wasn't her style. She would just say it out loud, "I'm the right woman for you." She pounded her chest. "Me! Not some—some arbitrary woman who doesn't even know that you like action movies, but you absolutely love watching romantic comedies. She doesn't know that your favorite food is Chinese, but you'd spend your last penny for Mexican food. She doesn't know that you make friends easily but you drop them if you even so much as detect a hint of disloyalty. You have high standards because you maintain them also."

"You..." He shook his head. "You..."

Obviously, he was incapable of speech. She could understand his quandary. But once he sat to ponder over this matter, he would eventually come to the same conclusion. They belonged together. "I love you, Fitz. And yes, I suppose I always have. It never occurred to me that you would be idiotic enough to fall for someone who is obviously not good for you. That woman will never know you like I know you. She'll never appreciate you as much as I do." She pointed a finger at him. "And yes, I'm pissed over the fact that you could sleep with me and still not realize that we're meant to be together, but I can forgive you." She winced. "Or at least, I'll try."

Much to her consternation, he began to laugh. After sitting on the couch, he held his head in both hands and guffawed out loud.

She resisted the overwhelming urge to punch him. Love didn't flourish with violence though, but he would be getting a punch if he didn't stop. Sure, he was having a hard time accepting this now—but wait till he analyzed the situation. As always, she was right.

Wasn't she?

What if her love was one sided? Maybe he didn't feel it. If that were true, she wouldn't know what to do. She just put herself right out there, vulnerable and naked. If he rejected her, she would be devastated. "Admit it, Fitz. "You love me."

"Janay, you're hilarious! Really—you are," he spoke as he was laughing.

She stomped over and loomed over him. "This isn't a joke."

"Well, I'm afraid the joke's on you, sweetie. There's no other woman in my life."

She narrowed her eyes. "What are you talking about? Who's the bimbo you think you're in love with?"

"The bimbo—well, the other woman is—you."

Janay was at a loss for words.

Fitz stood, walked over to her and gripped her arms. "Janay, I've never loved anyone but you. You're the only one who fits into my life. I've been mustering the courage to ask you out for years, but the timing was always wrong."

Happiness bloomed in her heart. Did she hear him right? He loved her? "The timing was right this time around. Why didn't you tell me?"

"I wanted you to realize on your own that we belong together. The outcome would have been different if I'd told you." He grinned. "And yes, I. Do. Love. You." His expression grew serious. "Janay, will you do me the honor of being more than my best friend?"

He loves me!

This was the best, most surprising piece of news she'd gotten in a long time. She wanted to jump up and down and perhaps do a wild, victory dance. But she was determined to keep a graceful façade. His gaze locked with hers and a fission of heat ran along her skin. *Damn!* He made her melt with his hot, sexy persona. *Forget the grace!* She would take what he offered and show the world how happy she was.

She grinned. "Yes, Fitz, yes." She couldn't help it. Her arms wound around his neck and she lifted her chin to brush a kiss over his lips. "This is the best Christmas ever and you're my Christmas gift."

"And you. Are. Mine."

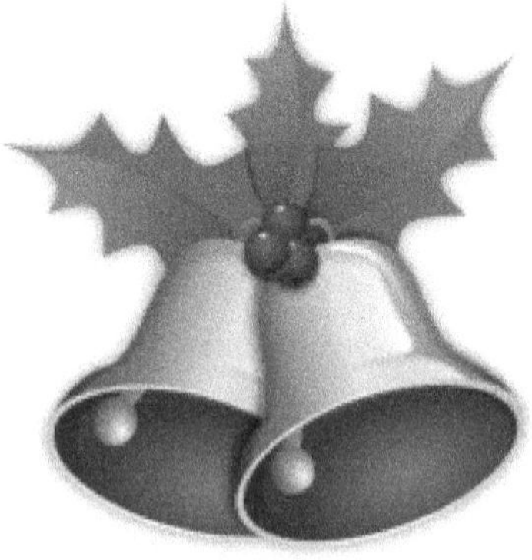

Chapter Ten

The concert was a huge success. The residents of the senior citizens' home really enjoyed listening to the music. Fitz stood next to the massive Christmas tree the sisters had decorated. Each person was to dispense a gift. Fitz insisted on contributing a few. He liked the fact that Janay and the others were committed to the residents of the home. Every Christmas they planned something big and different. That's what he loved about the woman; her dedication and commitment, her honesty, her go-get-it attitude and sheer nerves.

Lexi came to stand beside him. "So, how's your mom?"

"She's doing well. We've already hired a new resident housekeeper, so I'm feeling a bit relieved."

"I'm glad." Lexi's gaze was drawn to Cole who beckoned her. "Excuse me."

Fitz strolled in the opposite direction, towards the buffet table. It was time to swipe a dessert or two. He ran into Janay.

"Hey, handsome!" She put her hand on his arm. "Where are you going with that determined look in your eyes?"

"I was heading towards the dessert table, but now I've found something sweeter." He ran a finger over her soft cheek. Her skin felt warm, smooth and her hazel-green dress sizzled under the twinkling lights. It hugged all her curves and she had plenty of them. "When are we going home? I can't wait to rip this dress off you."

"Shush!" She glared at him and then giggled. "Right now, I can't give you what you have in mind, but for now…" She pointed right up at the mistletoe hanging from the roof on a string. "A kiss would do."

Fitz sighed as he bent his head. "And I thought you'd never ask." When his lips brushed across hers, he felt a familiar heat blaze into his veins. He could never get enough of her, not even if he lived and died a million times. Her arms curled around his neck in a possessive gesture. He deepened the kiss. His tongue thrust inside to taste every crevice and cranny of her mouth. Even as she pressed her body against his, he yearned for more. Her breath felt hot and her lips soft. His tongue mingled with hers in an erotic dance. They were both fused together for a long time, until Toby nudged into him.

"Dude, get a room."

Laughing, they separated. "Don't worry," Fitz assured him, "we will."

Janay pinched him on the arm and strode off, giggling.

Two hours later, she unlocked her door and they both stumbled inside the house. Drunk on their need for each other, they tugged at each other's clothes as they kissed their way further into the house. The air was heavy with passion, making it hard to breathe.

She kissed the pulse that beat at the base of his throat, teasing him with feathery touches of her soft lips. Her kisses fuelled the inferno inside of him, causing his throat to throb harder than it ever had. With the ferocity of a wild cat, she unbuttoned his shirt, leaving him shirtless in a blink. His shirt fell to the floor, baring his torso to her touch. His arms went behind her to undo her zipper. As pretty as the dress was, it was a barrier to the heights of pleasure they craved. She shrugged out of the fabric and let it drop to her feet. Their lips met again as she stepped out of the dress. Her hands went to his waistline and wasted no time in ridding him of his belt.

Now without a belt, his pants rode low on his waist.

"Love your v-line, babe," she moaned. "It's giving me life, and it's definitely a mouth-watering view." She bent low and brushed her warm lips there; then, she flicked out her tongue and swept it along his v-line, causing goose bumps to pepper his skin. She raised herself slowly, a smile crossing her lips. She reached for his bulge, and when she cupped it through his pants, he responded with a grunt. His hands snaked around her to pull her closer. She gasped, her chest flat against his. He trailed his fingers down her neck and along the side of her breast, his eyes trained on her cleavage. She melted into his touch and shuddered with need.

Longing pulsated within him, bright and fiery. Groaning, he pushed a hand through her thick mass of dark hair and lifted her off the floor, bridal style. She fit right in his arms, just as naturally as a key fit into a keyhole. While her legs hanged in the air as he carried her toward the bedroom, her arm wrapped around his neck and pulled him in for another kiss. He could feel her lips stretching into a smile as he kissed her back. He smiled too, momentarily breaking the kiss.

He carried her to the bedroom, leaving behind a trail of discarded clothes in the living room. The cozy bed called out to them once they stepped into the bedroom. It was a call he gladly answered. He advanced to the bed and lay her down as gently as a bridegroom would lay down his woman on their wedding night. Her eyes were trained on him, boring deep holes into him. She'd been staring at him like that the whole time he cradled her in his arms. Her eyes were wide and amorous, with a melting look that made him go weak at the knees. He knew the look in his eyes was just as intense. The change in her breathing pattern was enough proof of that. Her breaths were quick and shallow, and her heart rising and falling every split-second.

Fitz glided his fingers through her panty and slipped the flimsy fabric down her thighs. She moved her legs, seemingly eager to rid herself of the article of clothing. Once the underwear was out of the way, he bent to take a hard nipple into his mouth, and soon found himself mounting her, his body covering hers.

Her body arched under him and her fingers speared through his hair and tugged at it. Sucking and caressing, he fondled the swollen bud as she writhed under him. Her hands caressed his back and her fingernails dug deep into his skin, urging him to pick up pace. Fitz moved his attention to the other nipple even as his knee separated her legs. He moved his knee higher until it kissed the crux of her legs.

She gulped. Her throat throbbed, inviting him to kiss her right there. So he took a break from her nipple and straightened his neck. His lips found her throat, kissing her hard enough to knock the air out of her lungs. She gasped, out of breath. Her moaning voice grew thinner, close to a cry. Needing to hear more of that, he crushed his knee into her some more, tortuously teasing. When he straightened his leg, his erection brushed over her thigh. She moaned, her voice now brittle.

He buried his face between her twin mounds, panting with the need threatening to engulf him in its fiery embrace. Her fragrance, sweet and strong, hit his nostrils sweeping along every nerve, kindling a desire impossible to control.

God, but she was beautiful! He wanted to plunder and possess, worship her beauty, make her squirm and tremble until she screamed out his name.

As if answering his unspoken command, she whispered, "Fitz."

She reached down to undo his zipper. Her hands were quick, frantic, broadcasting her desperation to feel him inside her. He brought a hand to his waistband and helped her undress himself. His pants landed on the floor, and he positioned his hardness between her legs. She lay still, her stomach clenching and unclenching as she waited for him to claim his prize.

He sucked her nipple harder, rocking his body back and forth so his hardness glided back and forth between her legs. The squelching whispers of her moist opening were music to his ears, working alongside her moaning voice to fuel his raging hormones. Her moaning voice was soft and melodious, but despite its softness, it sought to overpower his deep groans.

He tugged at the curls that guarded her velvety center. He gorged on her breasts while he hovered over her moist opening. With a mighty push, he thrust deep inside, invading the darkest of places. She bucked under him, her eyes lighting up with triumph. Her tight walls were quick to adjust to his girth. They stretched around him as he stayed buried inside of her. His tongue flicked out to taste the beads of sweat that popped over her smooth, warm skin. She squeezed her eyes shut, and her thick long lashes started to flutter as she squirmed and moaned. Her lips stayed shut, trapping in her cries of her ecstasy.

Fitz couldn't wait anymore to have her. Not a moment longer!

He shifted onto his elbows and readjusted his body so his weight crushed her to the bed.

"Oh yes," she whispered, more to herself than to him.

He stroked in and out, slow at first. His pace was natural, easy to follow, so she moved her hips, matching him. He picked up pace with each thrust. She followed, her hips moving to meet his as he eased in and out of her. Soft whimpers escaped her when his thrusts seemed to become too intense for her. But she caught up with his relentless rhythm, meeting him thrust for thrust.

A sheen of sweat blanketed him. She was just as sweaty, but her arms around him kept him glued to her, even though their perspiration sought to drive them apart. Her nipples brushed against the hair on his chest, igniting a fire. Her eyes were glazed over while she moaned and raised her hips up against him.

Seeing she was close, he gave in to the urgent demands of his body. He rode her hard and good, his skin slamming into hers. The momentum built fast and strong while it carried him along a current of heat that swept through him. Janay's legs started to tremble, and so did her whole body. The sheets beneath her body had become a ruffled mess.

Fitz could feel all his energy gathering up in his cock. It spurred him to go harder. It was a command—one he couldn't object.

"Please..." Her voice was distant, brittle.

Was she begging him to go harder? Or was she begging him to go easy? He couldn't tell, but he concluded it was the former, so he pounded her harder, keeping up with a tortuous rhythm that made his heart threaten to burst out of his chest. Each breath came out as a pant. Passion. Need. Heat. Everything churned and curled in his gut, pulsing through his veins and exploding in his stomach. His primal urges kicked in. It was just him and her writhing body underneath him.

Nothing else mattered.

Her body trembled beneath him, begging for a release. He swirled inside of her, taking every inch of her constricting walls. She wrapped her legs around him and buried her face between his neck and shoulder.

"Now, baby! Now," she muttered.

For a long glorious moment, he swayed on the cusp of that tingling feeling, stretching the time as much as he could, until finally he was rewarded with a loud scream as an orgasm rippled through her. She shuddered under him and he whispered her name. His body grew rigid over hers. Fitz collapsed and they lay together, trying to quell their pacing hearts. He couldn't move and he didn't want to. Finally, he was right where he belonged and he didn't want to change a thing.

"I love you."

"I love you, too," he responded with a light kiss on her forehead.

Now, there was only one thing left to do.

And soon, they would get to it.

****

Two weeks later, Fitz checked his reflection in the mirror. Although he adjusted his tie, his gaze remained fixed on the milling crowd behind him. When he spotted his quarry, he turned and nudged Janay. "There she is."

They both stared at Arianna, the woman who was systematically destroying the livelihood of the three sisters, just to quench the fires of revenge burning deep in her heart.

Once Janay was sure what she wanted to do, she wasted no time in pursuing her goal. The Rogers cooperated fully and the sisters sprang into action to trap their nemesis. "I want to bash her on the head with something."

"Easy, baby, easy." He gripped her elbow. "Come, dance with me."

Without resisting, she went into his arms even as she signaled Brielle.

Fitz pulled her on to the dance floor. As she swayed along with him, her body fitting against his, Fitz felt relaxed. He knew his girl. Once she set her mind on a something, she hardly ever missed. In fact, he had counted on this very trait kicking in for all those weeks he worked on his, *get-Janay-into-his-arms* plan.

"The plan is set," she whispered.

"And you'll do a fine job of it."

"What if she doesn't confess?"

Bending his mouth close to her ear, he deposited a light kiss. "You'll make her, I'm sure of it." While she gazed into his eyes, Fitz couldn't quite comprehend how he could have been so lucky. Janay had always been the one for him. She completed him in ways that no other woman ever did. Now, that he had her, he would never let her go.

"That's my cue," she whispered when he led her off the floor and Brielle disappeared into the hallway. "Wish me luck."

"Good luck, baby. Go get her!"

Janay marched off to join her sisters.

Fitz followed at a more discreet pace. He didn't want to miss the fun. While the sisters waited beside the alcove that contained the house phone, he stood behind the pillar, so he couldn't be seen.

Arianna put the receiver down. She turned, saw them and flinched. Seeing that there was no escape, she squared her shoulders. "So, you guys lured me here with a false phone call?"

"It wasn't that difficult," Janay replied as she stood in the middle of her two elder sisters. "You've been bad-mouthing us, Arianna. So many lost contracts in two years. It's quite a big loss of potential profit, not to mention a dent in our reputation and good will."

Arianna's laugh sounded shrill. "And so, what if I did? You don't have any proof."

"I wonder what the police would think of it if we slap a lawsuit on you. After you got away with community service for doing what you did to Lexi, we thought you would've learned your lesson. Defaming someone is a serious offense."

"As I said, you don't have any evidence."

"But you did it."

Arianna lifted a dainty shoulder as her gaze shot to Lexi's stomach that was just beginning to show. "She stole my husband."

"He was never yours," Lexi shot back. "But he could have been. You left him at the altar just because you got cold feet. You didn't want to tie yourself to any man. But did you stop to think about what happened after you ditched him? You didn't even call to apologize."

"I made a mistake," Arianna whispered. Her body trembled as if she was fighting to control her temper. "And when I realized it and went to his house, I saw you both together. You were coming out of his building, holding hands, looking perfect together. That was supposed to me. ME! You took my place. I had no option but to spy on you both to see how serious things were. All I wanted was to drive you away from him by scaring you a bit. But you decided to stay. It wasn't my fault."

Janay glared at their archenemy. "And it wasn't your fault that you told people lies about us, about our work and the service we offer? You said that we were inconsistent, greedy, and manipulative."

"You're all that and more."

"You told potential clients we delivered sub-standard work."

Arianna laughed bitterly. "So what if I did?"

Janay took a step forward. "My sisters and I take pride in our work. We go above and beyond what our clients expect of us, and you damn well know it. Hell, everyone knows it!" Janay took another step towards Arianna, but Brielle put a hand on her shoulder, as if to hold her back. "So what, if you made a few clients run away. We have many more who are loyal. They'll stick around, no matter what you say or do. You won't be able to bring us down, so you may as well give up now. Or else, we'll stop you."

Arianna's laugh came out as spiteful. "And how are you going to do that?"

With a wicked grin, Janay pointed upwards. On the ceiling was a camera trained on Arianna. Its green blinking light showed that it captured every single word she said.

Arianna shifted her weight nervously. "That—is nothing."

"It's a good enough evidence for a defamation suit, if the girls decide to slap one on you." Fitz came out from behind a pillar, followed by Cole and Toby who'd joined him a while ago. The men looked as determined as the women of the group. "And we've already talked to all the people you told lies to and they'll be happy to testify against you in court. This time around, you won't get away with just community service."

"Cole!" Arianna stared into the eyes of the man she once claimed to love and then jilted on their wedding day. "I—I didn't mean any harm."

Cole walked forward and put his arm around his pregnant wife. "You never do, that's your problem, Arianna. But you need to accept blame or else you can't move forward. We want to put this in the past and get on with our lives. And you should do the same. There's no place in our lives for you."

As she stared at the three united couples, Arianna chewed on her bottom lip. Maybe she felt regret.

Although, Fitz doubted the woman was capable of such a genuine emotion.

Without exchanging another word, she strode past them and went back into the room where the party was still going on.

"I think she's gone for good this time," Janay said.

"Let's hope so." Fitz's eyes strayed to the camera which he'd help Toby to set up. It was his idea to confront the woman and make her see that she wouldn't get away with her bullying tactics. And they'd done just that. He felt pretty sure she wouldn't do it again. After all, her own reputation would be at stake now. She wouldn't want people to call her a liar and a fraud.

She was out of their lives now, and they all could concentrate on the good.

"Soon-to-be-wife, I think you owe me a dance," Toby said as he drew Brielle into his arms. "Come on. We'll set that place on fire."

Brielle giggled as she allowed him to whisk her away.

Cole sighed as he patted his wife's stomach. "We should take it easy, I suppose. Let's sit and eat something."

"I'm not hungry," Lexi quibbled.

"But I am," he countered in a good-natured way.

Soon, Janay and Fitz were left alone in the hallway. Fitz put his arms around her waist and drew her towards him. "You were magnificent. I heard it all. The woman never saw it coming."

"She should've been more careful." Janay rested her head on his shoulder. "But I'm glad that we did this."

"And I'm glad that we're together." He lifted her chin and touched his lips to hers. The kiss was soft and gentle and yet it birthed a yearning in his heart. It pulsed into his veins and nerves, binding her to him. "Forever and ever."

She kissed him.

It was just be the beginning of their amazing story.

The End

Did you miss the first book in this Holiday Happiness series, A Christmas Kiss? Then all you have to do is BUY YOUR COPY TODAY!

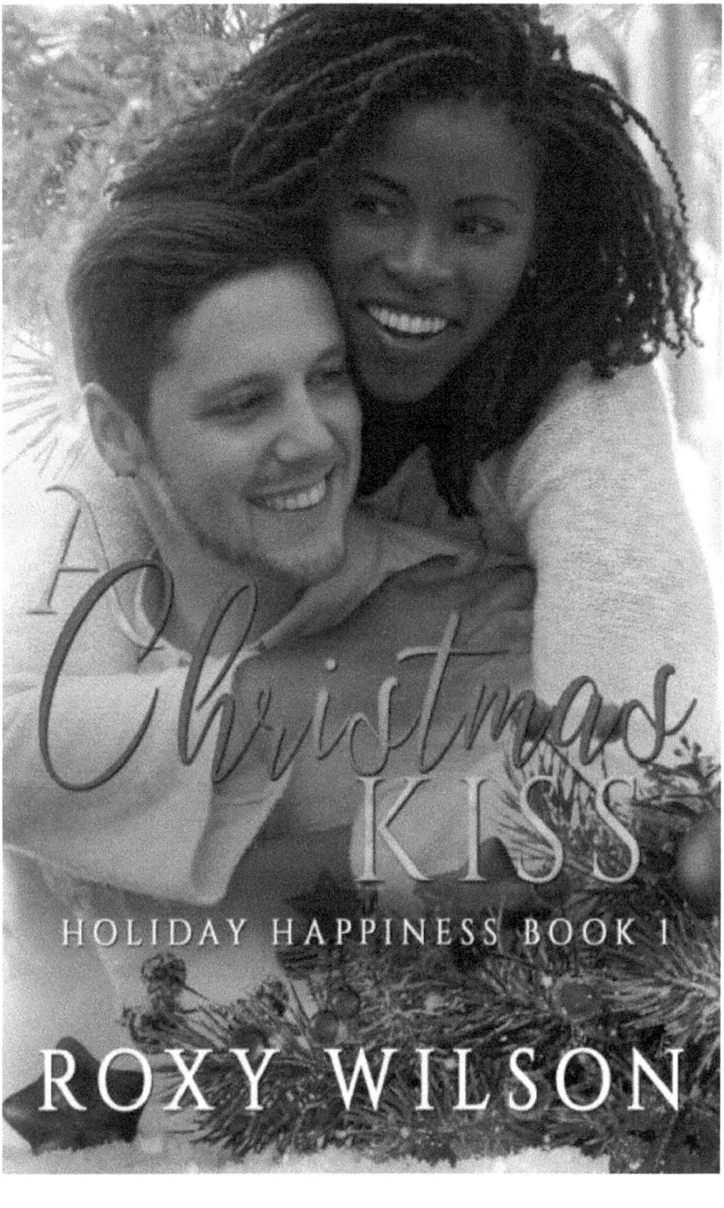
A Christmas KISS
HOLIDAY HAPPINESS BOOK 1
ROXY WILSON

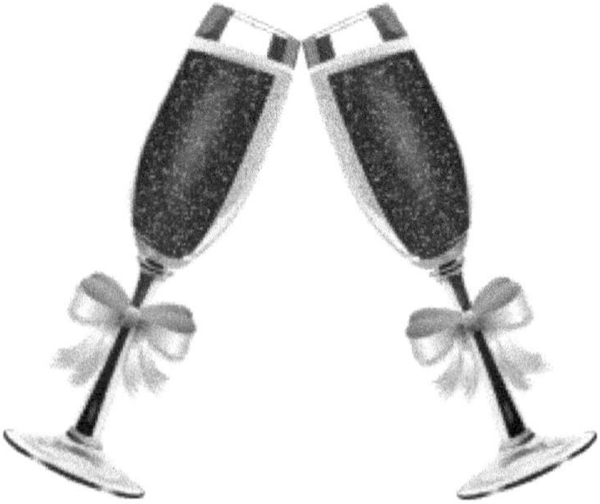

Chapter One

Lexi Riley didn't like surprises. In her line of work as the CEO of Riley's Grand Events, the event management company that she owned along with her two sisters, an untimely twist and turn could ruin a well-planned occasion. And that is why she always managed to tie every loose end, leaving nothing to chance. Every event organized by the three sisters was fabulous and beautiful, and this particular wedding would meet the strict standards she adhered to.

As she strode forward on her three-inch stiletto heels, Lexi monitored the activity. The guests were in place, the tables were set for the reception in the garden, her sister Brielle's mouthwatering food was ready to be served as soon the ceremony was over, and all she needed to do was enjoy the rest of the day.

Lexi scanned the area where the ceremony was to take place. It was Christmas Day, but she was pleased when the bride, Arianna, had agreed to move away from using the traditional Christmas colors and instead chose gold, burgundy, and forest-green. Lexi's eyes followed the trail of glitter stars and hearts that were placed on the floor to line the aisles. The pillar candles, enshrouded in clear glass cylinders, were placed strategically among the stars and hearts. Lexi beamed at the way the multi-colored glitter on the stars caught the candlelight and helped to highlight the Christmas ambience.

There might be hiccups later in the evening, but there was little that Lexi couldn't handle. Stopping at the mirror to check the exquisite floral arrangement, she removed a dead leaf that marred its beauty. *There. All perfect now!*

She gazed into the mirror and adjusted the sweeping, tiered skirt of her chiffon gown. With its halter neckline and finely pleated empire waist, the lavender dress accentuated her curves and brought a glow to her charcoal-black eyes. Her hair was tied in a neat chignon. She looked professional, yet elegant and feminine for the wedding.

If everything went well tonight, she could expect many more new clients from this lot. Her eyes scanned the guests, and she got a glimpse of a senator, a well-known businessman, and a TV personality in the crowd. Either the bride or the groom was well connected, and it wouldn't be a waste of time to wow them with the flawless preparations of Riley's Grand Events.

The earpiece she wore crackled. "Lexi!" hissed the youngest of the Riley sisters, Janay. "We've got a situation."

Lexi nearly huffed. "Don't tell me that the seating arrangement is messed up."

"No! That is all good."

So, what else could it be? "Is there a problem with the food? I saw Brielle an hour ago, and she assured me that everything was ready on her end."

"It's not the food," Janay said. She was the sister who took care of the company's finance and accounting department and also pitched in on actual events.

Lexi's mind raced. *What the heck is wrong, then*? "Spit it out, Janay."

Her sister expelled a deep breath. "The bride's missing."

The silence that followed Janay's pronouncement was so deafening that Lexi actually heard her heart pound. "Did you just say that the *bride* is missing?"

"Yes, she's not in her room. Her mother and sister have no idea where she is. I've looked everywhere and—"

"You've got to be joking." Lexi interrupted. It wasn't possible to conduct a wedding without a bride. How was she going to get this event rolling? "Tell me you're joking, Janay. Maybe she stepped out for a smoke or something."

"She doesn't smoke. And the guard at the gate assured me that he saw her getting into a cab about twenty minutes ago."

"What...Wait...Why didn't he stop her?"

"He didn't have the authority to do so. She's a client of the hotel."

"Shit! Shit! Shit! Shit!" Lexi nearly stomped her feet, something she never did. Maintaining a dignified and controlled persona at all times was critical, but just this once, she wished she could pull out her hair and bawl like a baby.

"Do you want me to announce to the guests that the wedding's off?"

"No!" Her thoughts scattered in all directions. She needed to get a handle on this situation. Lexi drew in a deep, controlled breath and released it slowly. Then she did it again. It was what she did whenever she needed to recover what little of her composure she could manage when things went terribly wrong. "Let me talk to the groom first. He's the one paying for this wedding. What did he say when you told him?"

"He doesn't know yet."

Lexi grimaced. This wasn't news that she wanted to deliver to anyone, not even to her worst enemy. But he was her client, and as such he deserved her support at this difficult time. She straightened her shoulders. "I'll tell him right now."

"Do you want me to go with you?" Janay said in a voice that suggested she would rather be anywhere else than with her big sister for this task.

Lexi didn't think he would appreciate an audience. "No, I'll manage. Until I give the okay, don't utter a word to anyone."

"Yes, of course."

Lexi clicked off. Without wasting a moment, she marched off towards the gate to speak with the guard. She didn't want to tell the groom anything until she was a hundred percent sure her sister wasn't wrong. Not that Janay ever was, but these particular circumstances called for special measures, and she didn't want to leave anything to chance. Lexi took her time to check each nook and corner of the hotel. Of course, she couldn't peek into each room, but short of that, she made her staff search for the bride in every place they could think of. Once she was sure of the facts, she headed off towards the room where the groom was waiting with his best man. When she put her hand on the handle, Lexi took a deep breath and ordered herself to calm down. She knocked and entered after being summoned inside.

The bride must have a few loose marbles, Lexi thought as she cast her eyes on the groom. Cole Davenport took her breath away from the first moment she'd seen him when he came with his bride-to-be—now the runaway bride—several months earlier for their first consultation. His warm, caramel-colored hair was cut short, his electric-blue eyes were startlingly bright, and his face was just shy of movie-star handsome. But it was the scar above his right eye that drew her attention. It was the mark of a man who'd fought his battles in a war and won against all odds. He was a retired army captain and now an author of best-selling psychological thrillers and mysteries. It was all Lexi knew about him. And now, she'd find out soon enough if he deserved the medal that his fiancée—ex-fiancée—told her he earned because of his exploits in the war against terrorism.

And from what Lexi had seen, based on her interactions with him as they prepared for the wedding, he seemed to be a really decent guy.

Yep, Arianna was crazy to walk away from the man that was Cole Davenport. In fact, there was something about her that Lexi couldn't quite put her finger on, but it always left her uneasy in Arianna's presence. Sure, she seemed a bit selfish, pretentious, and spoiled, which was probably expected since she was born and raised in the lap of luxury. But there was something not quite stable about her. Whenever Arianna visited her office to discuss the wedding preparations, Lexi always got the impression that she was just going through the motions. From Lexi's experience, as the wedding day drew nearer, the brides-to-be were usually gushing with enthusiasm or panicking or a combination of both extremes. But Arianna was different. Eerily so. Oftentimes, Lexi mentally shrugged her shoulders and reasoned that she was perhaps too critical of Arianna; but judging by Arianna's stunt today, it seemed as if Lexi wasn't far off base. Now she had to concentrate on the task at hand: breaking the news to Mr. Davenport about his runaway bride-to-be.

"Mr. Davenport?"

When Cole's gaze settled on her, she resisted the urge to retrace her steps and leave the room. Nothing in her line of work prepared her to handle this kind of situation. She needed help. But there was no one who could bail her out. And in any case, Lexi Riley wasn't a coward.

"Yes?"

"I'd like to talk to you in private."

He frowned. "Isn't it time for us to get started? Don't tell me my bride isn't ready, yet."

"Arianna has never been ready on time." The best man laughed. "Your military precision is going to suffer a lot now, Cole. You'll always be late for every event, including your own wedding."

Lexi folded her arms and tapped her foot against the tiled floor. She didn't have time for fun and games. She directed a cool stare at the best man. "Excuse me, sir. I'd really like to talk to Mr. Davenport alone."

The best man stared at her for a moment, as if trying to weigh the seriousness of her words. Then he shrugged, exchanged a quick glance with the groom, and left them alone. When Lexi was sure the door was closed, she made a show of walking calmly toward the man in the room until she was standing directly in front of him. If he collapsed after she broke the news to him, she'd make every attempt to catch him, but it wouldn't be an easy feat. He was about two or three inches above six feet, and she knew from seeing him in more casual clothes that his shoulders were broad and his limbs were muscular, though not overly so. And with his military background and the way he kept his physique even though he was no longer in active duty, she knew that Mr. Davenport not only looked strong, he was strong. She figured she might not be able to hold him upright, but she might be able to save him from banging his head on the tiled floor.

She cleared her throat. "Umm...Mr. Davenport, I've got some bad news."

He cocked his head to the side. "Is there a problem with the payment?"

She felt terrible. He'd already cleared the bill. What was she supposed to do in this particular, disastrous situation? Should she return his money?

First things first.

Lexi took a deep breath and then released slowly. "It's not about the money. Unfortunately, we can't find the bride."

For one minute, he simply stared at her. "Can't find her? What do you mean?"

"She's not in the hotel."

"But the wedding is about to start. Where could she have gone?"

Lexi placed a hand on his arm. "I'm afraid that she may have left on purpose."

"What the hell are you talking about?"

She gulped. He clearly wasn't able to comprehend the gravity of her words. Lexi chose her next sentence with care. "I'm afraid that she may have decided that she doesn't want to get married."

"Have you lost your mind?" Cole dragged his fingers through his hair. "We're about to get married," he said, glancing down at his watch, "in five minutes. She can't just decide to walk away. This must be some mistake." He began to pace the length of the room.

Lexi's eyes tracked his movements. "I've searched the place, Mr. Davenport. Why don't you give her a call to see if she picks up?"

He stopped in his tracks as he seemed to latch on to her suggestion with the efficiency of a desperate man. Thrusting his hand inside his pocket, he took out his cell phone and dialed. Lexi wrung her hands together, silently pleading with the runaway bride-to-be to pick up the phone. She mentally made the sign of the cross when she saw a smile lit Mr. Davenport's face.

"Arianna, honey, where are you?"

When the smile slipped, Lexi wished she was far away. At least the woman had the decency to talk to him, even if it was over the phone. She shivered when he began pacing the room again. "But why?"

When he slipped the phone back into his pocket and just stood there, Lexi didn't know what to do. The clock in the room ticked. Outside, a bird twittered. Still, he didn't move.

"Mr. Davenport? Guests are already waiting in the chapel. What would you like me to do?"

"She doesn't want to get married," he said as if he didn't hear her question. "Not to me, at least."

Lexi didn't think this was a good time to ask him if the bride-to-be had chosen another groom. Some women got cold feet at the altar, as did some men, but she'd never coordinated a wedding in which one of them deserted the other. "Mr. Davenport? Is there anything I can do for you?"

"What?"

"Is there anything I can do for you?" she repeated.

He ran his hands through his hair. "Oh dear god! The guests!"

"If you like, I could announce that...the wedding has been put off for an unforeseeable future."

"Future?" He stared at Lexi as if she'd lost her mind. "I don't have a future. My fiancée decided to leave me rather than exchange vows. I don't know why. She wouldn't give me an explanation."

"I'm sorry, Mr. Davenport." Lexi wrung her hands together again. What the hell was she supposed to do? Luckily, he didn't faint. "Would you like some time to be by yourself?"

He focused on her. "Damn."

Once again, she was rendered speechless. Lexi wasn't sure if she should leave him alone. If she were in his shoes, she'd want someone by her side, even if that person was an impersonal employee, or well, sort of. Maybe she needed to call the best man back and let him deal with the groom. After all, that should be part of his job, not hers. But seeing the anguished look in Cole's eyes, she didn't think she could leave him yet. He certainly wouldn't want someone to see him like this, even if that person was his best friend. Perhaps being with a stranger would ease his pain a bit.

Lexi reached over and rubbed his arm. She almost pulled away from him when she felt the shiver of awareness.

Come on, Lexi, you've got to focus.

"Mr. Davenport. I'll do whatever I can to ease this situation. If you want, you could leave the venue and we'll take care of this. The food is ready, the guests can be served, and we can just tell them that there was an emergency."

Much to her shock, he gripped her arm, drew her toward himself, and claimed her lips...

BUY[1] NOW!
https://books2read.com/u/3nWzdB

---

1. https://www.amazon.com/Christmas-Kiss-Romance-Holiday-Happiness-ebook/dp/B082J4MCHV/africanamericanromance

Did you miss the second book in this Holiday Happiness series, Second Chance Christmas? Then all you have to do is to BUY your copy TODAY!

SECOND CHANCE Christmas

HOLIDAY HAPPINESS BOOK 2

ROXY WILSON

BLURB

Caterer Brielle Riley-Foster can't believe her luck when she runs into her ex-husband, Toby, at a pre-Christmas party. Four years after he suddenly filed for divorce, her heart still pines for him and the pain of losing him still sears.

For Toby, the sight of his ex-wife brings back the sting he felt when she cheated on him. Unwilling to let her back into his life, Toby does his best to avoid contact, but Brielle has cooked up a scheme that is sure to make her indiscretion pale in comparison.

Her desperate attempt to make her ex-husband answer her long-held questions isn't winning her any sanity points, and things get worse when heavy snow begins to fall and old hurts resurface. With no way out, the exes are forced to communicate with each other and soon discover some surprising things, things they never expected.

Has too much time passed for Brielle and Toby to find their way back to one another, or is this love lost for good?

Here's a sneak peek...

Chapter One

The pre-Christmas party was in full swing. Brielle Riley-Foster surveyed the scene in the kitchen. She was tired, yet fulfilled, and happy that everything was organized with military precision. Rarely did she ever lose her cool. And even now, as she observed the bustling activity, she didn't become flustered. While the waiters carried out appetizers of sautéed black olives with tomatoes, bacon-wrapped dates, cucumber-rye tea sandwiches, lamb pizzettes, miso-glazed smoked sable on rice crackers, and spicy pecans, and the chef bellowed for more spices for the main course, she remained calm. She inhaled deeply, delighting in the heady aroma of the marmalade-glaze roast turkey, ham with five-spice cherry sauce, and the beef tenderloin with Parmesan-herb stuffing. This fare would surely delight meat lovers. She lifted lids and checked to make sure that the side dishes—jerked-spiced Brussels sprouts and cauliflower, chickpea, and warm mushroom salad—were to her specifications. A delicious warmth spread throughout her body. As always, her food was up to standards and she didn't have any doubt that those she trained would do their jobs with her trademark efficiency.

The tap-tapping of heels, announced Janay's arrival, the youngest of the Riley sisters. She was the one who inherited all the temper in the family. And even now she looked disturbed, a sheen of sweat visible on her forehead.

"What's wrong?" said Brielle.

"There's an additional guest," she hissed.

Brielle raised a hand towards her chef. "John. We've got one addition." She turned to look at her sister. "There. Problem solved. We'll be able to serve him or her without a hitch."

"But what about the seating arrangement?"

"That's not my department," said Brielle. "Ask Lexi. She's the one who's in charge of seating."

"I'll go find her." Janay drew in a deep breath and then expelled it slowly. "Why can't the hosts plan better?" she muttered. "Inviting unexpected people at the last minute is a recipe for disaster."

Brielle smiled to herself as she took a tray from one of her waiters and sauntered out. Dismissing Janay's concerns, she entered the dining room. Although she was the one who handled the catering, once in a while, she preferred to mingle with the guests and see their reaction to the cuisine herself. Regarding the extra guest, she had no doubt that her competent sister, Lexi, would be able to manage things on her end.

It was Lexi's idea to establish Grand Events with all three sisters, a company that had already acquired an excellent reputation in the past four years. Quietly Brielle served, observing the guests and their preferences for her food as she made her way through the hall where the pre-Christmas party was being held.

As she glanced at the men and women who were dressed in their finery, her gaze stopped on a familiar figure. The hair at the back of her neck stood on end. Her breathing quickened. Her pulse raced. The tray wobbled in her hand. For the first, in a long time in her life, she actually felt dizzy. Pain, like a hard punch, hit her in the gut.

She sucked in a deep breath of air and scanned the room. She clutched the arm of the waiter who was making his way back into the kitchen. "Nick, here take this." She handed over the items she carried to the bewildered waiter, who ended up with two trays, and hurried away. She needed to get away. To compose herself.

Lexi, the eldest of the Riley sisters, was conferring with the chef. She glanced up and smiled when she saw Brielle entering in. "Hey, Brielle, the hostess said to delay serving the main course, because he wants to take photographs first." She gestured to the chef that still stood by her side. "I've told Tony to go slow with his preparations. We don't want to serve cold food."

Brielle barely took note of what Lexi was saying. Her brain was muddled. She was vaguely aware that her gait was sluggish since her feet were heavy, as if they belonged to someone else. She hoped her sister was finished with her briefing.

"...And guess what?"

No such luck.

"...The Johnsons called," Lexi continued. "They cancelled their event that was scheduled for next week." She frowned. "Apparently, they found someone else to manage it. They wouldn't give me any reason."

Brielle opened her mouth to respond, but her throat was dry. She swallowed and tried again, but still no words could escape her lips. Without saying a word, Brielle crossed through, opened the door of the storeroom, and stepped inside. The noise faded as she closed the door. But a moment later, her sister walked in.

"What's wrong?" she demanded. "You look like you've seen a ghost."

"He's here."

Lexi frowned. "Who's here?"

"Toby," she was aware that she spat out the word as if it was dirt stuck in her mouth.

Lexi slumped against the wall. "Here? In this party?" Her gaze flittered around as if searching for the object of their discussion. "But...I thought he left town after your divorce."

Brielle rubbed a hand on her forehead, which was clammy with sweat. "He left...but I guess he's back."

Her husband of two years walked out on her without an explanation or a word about four years ago. A month later, she received the notice of divorce in the mail. Despite her best attempts to contact him, she couldn't get through. He'd left the country and had carried out all of the divorce proceedings through his lawyers. Even now, when she thought back to the callous treatment she got, her heart clenched with pain. How could he break up their marriage without telling her the reason for it? She'd made calls, sent emails, pestered his parents, wrote letters, sat in his lawyer's office for hours, but there was no response. No one knew the reason why he wanted the marriage to end. And the one person who could answer her question was not in the country.

The action was so uncharacteristic for him that it shook her to her core. He wasn't the sort of man who shed his responsibilities without care. He was the man you could depend on, lean on in times of need, and take support from. Whatever made him change his mind about their future and marriage must have been momentous. But what was it? And why didn't he tell her? When she didn't get answers, Brielle moved on, albeit with a great deal of difficulty.

And now, he was back. And damn it! He looked just as handsome...

BUY NOW!
https://books2read.com/u/3kW70R

THANK YOU!

Thank you for taking a chance on *CHRISTMAS CUPID* and trusting me to give you a few hours of reading pleasure. I'd be happy if you do me a favor. Many potential readers depend on honest reviews to determine if they should 1-Click a book. Please help them make an informed decision by posting a review of *CHRISTMAS CUPID*. Your review doesn't have to be long.

I love hearing from readers, so you may shoot me an email to author.roxywilson@gmail.com. That's how our friendship will begin, if we aren't friends already.

I also hope you'll consider joining my mailing list. By doing this, you'll receive updates on my upcoming releases, giveaways, deals and free reads. It will surely be an honor if you decide to subscribe. To join my mailing list, visit https://dl.bookfunnel.com/ecwew3qpox.

Kind regards, always!

Roxy

Sign up for news, new release alerts, giveaways, free reads, ARC opportunities and so much more

https://dl.bookfunnel.com/ecwew3qp0x

Shoot me an email at:

author.roxywilson@gmail.com

Books by Roxy Wilson

Dark Romance

Alessandro Mancini - https://books2read.com/u/mqr291

Holiday Romance

A Christmas Kiss - https://books2read.com/u/3nWzdB

Second Chance Christmas - https://books2read.com/u/3kW70R

Christmas Cupid - https://books2read.com/u/mdnPrW

About the Author

Roxy Wilson, a self-professed book junkie, was born and bred in a beautiful island in the Caribbean.

When Roxy isn't reading or writing, she spends her time trying out recipes with her daughter, designing and dress making, listening to music of the 80's and 90's or engaging in her favorite workout routine, which is 1-clicking a new book to read, to her heart's content.

Want to be notified of any new releases, giveaways, deals and free reads? Sign up for Roxy Wilson's mailing list now! Want to be notified of any new releases, giveaways, deals and free reads? Sign up for Roxy Wilson's mailing list now! Click https://dl.bookfunnel.com/ecwew3qpox.

Don't miss out!

Visit the website below and you can sign up to receive emails whenever Roxy Wilson publishes a new book. There's no charge and no obligation.

https://books2read.com/r/B-A-UMO-LZUKB

BOOKS 2 READ

Connecting independent readers to independent writers.